POLISH(ED)

Poland Rooted in Canadian Fiction

To Dearest Irenka
with admiration
& hugs
Anna Miodek

K.J.

ESSENTIAL ANTHOLOGIES SERIES 10

**Canada Council
for the Arts**

**Conseil des Arts
du Canada**

ONTARIO ARTS COUNCIL
CONSEIL DES ARTS DE L'ONTARIO

an Ontario government agency
un organisme du gouvernement de l'Ontario

Canadä

Guernica Editions Inc. acknowledges the support of the Canada Council
for the Arts and the Ontario Arts Council. The Ontario Arts Council
is an agency of the Government of Ontario.

We acknowledge the financial support of the Government of Canada.

POLISH(ED)

Poland Rooted in Canadian Fiction

Edited by
Kasia Jaronczyk
&
Małgorzata Nowaczyk

GUERNICA
EDITIONS
TORONTO • BUFFALO • LANCASTER (U.K.)
2017

Kasia Jaronczyk and Małgorzata Nowaczyk, editors
Michael Mirolla, general editor
David Moratto, cover and interior design
Guernica Editions Inc.
1569 Heritage Way, Oakville, (ON), Canada L6M 2Z7
2250 Military Road, Tonawanda, N.Y. 14150-6000 U.S.A.
www.guernicaeditions.com

Distributors:
University of Toronto Press Distribution,
5201 Dufferin Street, Toronto (ON), Canada M3H 5T8
Gazelle Book Services, White Cross Mills
High Town, Lancaster LA1 4XS U.K.

First edition.
Printed in Canada.

Legal Deposit—Third Quarter
Library of Congress Catalog Card Number: 2017932203
Library and Archives Canada Cataloguing in Publication
Polish(ed) : Poland rooted in Canadian fiction / edited by Kasia Jaronczyk
and Małgorzata Nowaczyk.

(Essential anthologies ; 10)
Issued in print and electronic formats.
ISBN 978-1-77183-144-4 (softcover).--ISBN 978-1-77183-145-1
(EPUB).--ISBN 978-1-77183-146-8 (Kindle)
1. Poland--Civilization--Fiction. 2. Poland--Social life and customs--Fiction.
3. Canadian fiction (English)--21st century. 4. Poland--In literature. 5. Polish
people in literature. I. Jaronczyk, Kasia, editor II. Nowaczyk, Małgorzata,
editor III. Series: Essential anthologies series (Toronto, Ont.) ; 10
PS8323.P67P65 2017   C813'.608035299185   C2017-900582-0   C2017-900583-9

POLISH(ED)

Poland Rooted in Canadian Fiction

Contents

Preface

A collection of Polish-Canadian writing has been Kasia's dream for a long time. During her first years in Canada she never thought it would be possible to come from a different culture, from a different language, and to write in a new country, in a language other than her mother tongue. Margaret, busy establishing herself in Canadian realities, never even gave writing a passing thought—it just wasn't practical. They both knew of writers who have done it successfully and in the process pushed English literature and language to new heights, but they were geniuses like Vladimir Nabokov and Joseph Conrad. Kasia decided to become a microbiologist and pursued PhD studies while Margaret, convinced that her newly-acquired English would not get her far in any field other than science, chose medicine. Had they known of successful Polish-Canadian authors back then their lives might have turned out differently.

In spite of their chosen careers, they have always been searching for Polish-Canadian voices. They wanted to find a cultural connection, a common experience, someone who would show them that first generation immigrants could become successful writers in Canada. For both of them—even though they didn't know each other at the time and are fifteen years apart in age, the first two such voices were Eva Hoffman's *Lost in Translation*, and Eva Stachniak's *Necessary Lies*. But their experiences with those books were polar opposites: Kasia received *Lost in Translation* as a gift from her high school English as a Second Language teacher, Mrs. Jessie Porter, while Margaret was told by her Grade 11 English teacher that, even if she became bilingual, her English would never be idiomatic. She found *Lost in Translation* on her own in a Chicago bookstore years later. Reading *Necessary Lies* inspired Kasia to pursue a B.A. in English concurrently with her science degree, but it made Margaret regret not having started to write sooner. Throughout, they felt culturally and linguistically dispossessed and struggled to find a home in a new language. But, with time, reading books written by Polish immigrants to Canada gave them hope that they could also become Canadian writers. With the passing years, they discovered more Polish-Canadian authors. There was Ania Szado, whose *Beginning of Was* Kasia found by chance, or fate, in a small bookstore in Edmonton. More recently, Aga Maksimowska's *Giant*, a novel that tells the story of a girl of Kasia's generation who emigrated to Canada; *Copernicus Avenue* by Andrew J. Borkowski; Jowita Bydlowska's *Drunk Mom*; and Eva Stachniak's historical novels provided inspiration. For Kasia and Margaret these books—novels, short stories, memoirs —became an impetus to write. And they are both thrilled that these authors responded to the submission call for this anthology as enthusiastically as they did.

This is the first Polish diaspora collection published in Canada. There are collections of stories written by Canadian writers of African descent, by South-Asian Canadians, by Jewish-Canadian women, by Hungarian-Canadians. Within Canada, there are short story collections from Quebec, the Maritimes, the prairies, and the far North that showcase the cultural diversity of Canadian literature. But until now, the Polish diaspora was not represented among them. There are writers, such as Michael Ondaatje, Nino Ricci, Rohinton Mistry, Anita Rau Badami, Wayston Choy, whose names are often synonymous with writing from the diaspora they represent. There isn't a Polish-Canadian writer with this mantle. Yet.

When we approached Polish-Canadian authors about the idea of a Polish-Canadian anthology, their response was generous, enthusiastic, and inspiring. We have found a wonderful community of writers who, although they write in different styles and on different subjects, support each other and are proud to represent Poland on the Canadian literary map. We have received an astonishing number of submissions, many more that we were able to accept. In the process we have discovered emerging and established Canadian authors who include being Polish as part of their identity. A number of writers in the anthology are of Polish-Jewish heritage, which reflects the long common history of these two cultures.

This collection is by no means exhaustive or complete. The anthology includes Katarzyna Jaśkiewicz, Mark Bondyra, S.D. Chrostowska, Zoe Greenberg, David Huebert, Katherine Koller, Dawid Kołoszyc, Anna Mioduchowska, Lilian Nattel, Douglas Schmidt and Norman Ravvin—all writers for whom Poland has a meaning if not as a native land then as a land of their ancestors. And, since Polish-themed works are on the rise on the Canadian literary scene, this collection includes stories by Canadian authors who don't have Polish roots, but whose writing, however, contains Polish elements: Corinne Wasilewski, Christijan Robert Broerse, Lisa McLean, Pamela Mulloy, and Robert Young. Many of the authors included in this anthology have debuted or published new works in the last five years. Several are in the process of publishing their first novels, while Lilian Nattel, Eva Stachniak and Ania Szado have penned international bestsellers.

What is the literary and cultural benefit of a diaspora anthology? It presents work from a community, a family of writers. It represents a contribution to Canadian literature. It makes known where we come from personally and metaphorically, what inspires us. In our case, we are all writers who share Polish-ness, in whatever way we define it, as a part of our personal story, be it through similar experiences, influences, and perspective on the world, a sense of history and of who we are. And also, through interest in Polish diaspora, in the case of writers who have no Polish roots. A Polish diaspora anthology gives us a sense of pride, to see what we, as people coming from the same culture, have accomplished in another culture, and how similar and different we are in what and how we write. There exists in us a primal desire to find "our people"—people who are similar to us, and that is especially important to first generation writers like us. A diaspora collection offers a sense of belonging, a community, and role models for writers beginning to write in a new language.

We are grateful to Michael Mirolla, Connie McParland and Guernica Editions for supporting this project, and proud to present the first collection of Polish-themed contemporary fiction by Canadian writers. We hope that the readers will be encouraged to seek out and read other works of the authors included in its pages.

—Kasia Jaronczyk & Małgorzata Nowaczyk

Guelph & Hamilton, January 2016

Foreword

PALIMPSEST IDENTITY: POLISH-CANADIAN LINGUISTIC CONDITION

Our present age is one of exile.
—JULIA KRISTEVA[1]

The limits of my language mean the limits of my world.
—LUDWIG WITTGENSTEIN[2]

Language is one of the least noticeable, yet at the same time one of the strongest links between our internal life and *who we think we are* on the one hand, and the way we function in the outside world and interact with the fellow human beings on the other. Whenever we move to a new territory, whether physically or emotionally, we carry with us the baggage of experience that is stored in the form of sensory and, more often than not, verbal memories. Without those memories—images, feelings, voices and words, we would not be who we are. Thus the languages we grew up with and know well are factors in the process of identity construction. Until they are replaced by a new medium, they continue to serve as filters between us and the others. We realise the importance of language only when the link between the world and our internal linguistic representation of it is called into question, for instance when we leave our country and enter a new "life in a new language"[3].

---

1. Julia Kristeva, "A New Type of Intellectual: the Dissident," in: Toril Moi (ed.), *The Kristeva Reader* (London: Blackwell, 1986).

2. Ludwig Wittgenstein. 1922. Tractatus Logico-Philosophicus. 5.6

3. This is a reference to the second part of the title of Eva Hoffman's book *Lost in Translation: Life in a New Language.*

There is no universal scenario for *exile*. It may be understood as any kind of displacement, voluntary departure or compulsory expulsion from one's native land, expatriation, or simply, as many Poles came to realise, finding oneself outside the borders of one's native land, not because one had moved abroad but because the borders had moved. One may feel displaced, exiled and alienated by moving to a territory where the same language is spoken, but with a different accent, as accent too plays a role in the construction of identity.

The general terms *exile* or *displacement* apply to millions of people world-wide, and yet no two experiences of exile are similar enough to warrant the creation of a prototype of exile or of an expatriated individual. Even immigrants from one country of origin settling down in one new host country hardly ever form a homogeneous group. Poles in Canada are no exception.

However, no matter how different the experience and the mode of leaving the familiar territory, no matter whether one is allowed to take all of their belongings or is lucky to escape alive, there is one thing all displaced individuals take with them: their language (or languages). With language comes a representation of the native culture in the form of verbalised beliefs and traditions. Is it possible to retain this culture and these languages if one is physically removed from their sphere of influence and cut off from their roots? Is one doomed to lose touch with one's native culture and language by the very fact of being immersed in another one? Is it at all possible to free oneself from one's old identity and adopt a new language and a new set of cultural values? Is exile the worst fate imaginable, the way it was thought of by Euripides? Why then do so many people choose it again and again, voluntarily abandoning their native countries and searching for a better life in a Promised Land?

Language is so closely intertwined with all aspects of our identity that it may at times seem inseparable from it. One often equates national identity with the ability to speak the national language. Individual identity too is strongly related to language and so "the loss of one's language" could be seen as a loss of identity. This suggests that the ability to speak several languages could offer more than one way of self-presentation. That in turn would imply that a multilingual and multicultural individual has several *faces*, or, at the very least, that his repertoire of choices is more diverse and could be fine-tuned to a greater variety of cultural contexts.

Canada, which defines itself as a multicultural country, spanning the entire continent, *mari usque ad mare*, is a rather peculiar place for exile. It allows one to freely construct his identity and makes no impositions, but on the other hand, it does not offer any shortcuts to help immigrants integrate into mainstream Canadian society. No special invitation is extended to immigrants encouraging them to adapt or to become truly Canadian, as "being Canadian" is not a well-defined concept itself. While everyone is free to remain true to his or her own inner-self, foreign accents are not ridiculed and no Polish jokes are told, speaking "good English" is recognized as one of the means to power. In this way, one becomes a Canadian relatively easily, but never completely. This situation might be one of the reasons why Polish writing in Canada is not very visible. Perhaps there is no drama that would inspire creativity. We all live here as hyphenated nationalities: Polish-Canadians among Italian-Canadians, German-Canadians or Ukrainian-Canadians. For some, this double identification with cultures and tongues may be the constituting factor of being Canadian.

Many metaphors have been used to describe the experience of being displaced: some see exile as crossing over to a new territory, one which could be the Promised Land but which could also become an inferno. Some see it as death, others as rebirth. In her autobiographical book *Lost in Translation: A Life in a New Language*, Eva Hoffman, who at the age of thirteen left Poland for Canada, paints the picture of immigrating into a new language as a kind of self-translation.

There are various levels of language and identity loss, from the inability to communicate at all to the inability to communicate at the same level of sophistication as in the native language. Except for bilingual individuals, few people ever feel that they have reached the same proficiency in the new language. It may be that the high level of education in the native language adds to the difficulty of assimilation, as the gap between one's ability for self-projection in the two languages seems impossible to bridge.

We could approach the topic of the *loss* of one's native language as a challenge of finding a new voice that would allow us to express our identity through a new medium. Something is always lost in translation, but not everything, and a lot can be *found*, discovered or rediscovered about ourselves in this process, and *saved*. If only we are prepared to make an effort, the *loss* turns into *reconstruction* and language becomes a medium for finding a new self, or a new sense of self.

Language use and language behaviour define, to a large extent, an individual in the eyes of others. In the old country, the exile may no longer fit in linguistically and socially. In the new environment, he or she will likely continue to be perceived as foreign. The question of finding a new voice or a new self in the context of exile is of particular importance to people who work with language. Their professional identity is manifested through the medium of language and any changes to that medium distort their identity. And yet, it is often the writers, like Czesław Miłosz or Eva Hoffman who show us that moving away from their native language proved not to be an obstacle in their artistic development. Perhaps it was the very fact of being removed from the natural source of signs to label the reality that helped them develop a fine sense of insight into the mechanisms of language. This ability, or even necessity, to question things that others take for granted is perhaps the reward for the discomforts of displacement. It may also be what underlies the formation of an immediate, yet difficult to define bond between displaced persons, irrespectively of their origin and language.

We cannot keep our *self* or our identity intact, whether we stay at home or wander far away from it. Our identities change all the time, like everything around us. And where actually is "home" in this constantly changing world of ours? Don't we always try to make ourselves at home wherever we just happen to find ourselves? Are we not always on the way home?

While I move from one country to another, my identity changes like the seasons, adapts to places, people and situations the same way I dress for the weather. No one can take it away from me, but neither am I able to discard it. I cannot take it off, like a dress that has worn out, and replace it with a new one. As it is all I possess, I have to adapt it or alter it, carefully choosing accessories to fit the place and occasion. There are different things I talk about or keep silent about in Canada, different in Poland, and still different somewhere else. Even a simple question "How are you?" calls for different answers in different languages. Is this hypocrisy or lack of patriotic values or is it just the flexible nature of my identity, which, like the parchment of a medieval palimpsest, endures endless auto-corrections? Sometimes I have to remove a stain from it, erase something, scratch off with a knife some habits of my old self that make normal life in the new environment impossible. The palimpsest on which my identity is recorded endures those interventions, wounds close and heal and I can continue to write my life history in the 1st Person Singular in whichever language happens to best fit the purpose of communication.

Today's world is a scene of large-scale migrations of individuals and entire ethnic groups, who are forced to move away from their traditional homeland by wars, ethnic unrest, environmental disasters and economic factors. This makes the more individualistic word *exile* sound almost elitist. Most people move because they face extermination or extinction. We should remember this when we talk about exile, language and identity. We are discussing the implications of the loss of language and identity in exile, which really is a luxury when so many people lose not just their identities but lives.

—MAGDA STROIŃSKA

Department of Linguistics and Languages, McMaster University

Based on "The role of language in the re-construction of identity in exile" by M. Stroińska and V. Cecchetto in *Exile, Language and Identity* (Peter Lang, editor), Frankfurt am Main. 2003.

ICEBERG

Aga Maksimowska

WHEN THE BOY walked Molly home from the pub, her husband was asleep with their dog nuzzled into his lower back. Dr. Watson, the Giant Schnauzer, had his paw on Mike's waist; he was spooning Mike like Molly used to. Molly didn't want the boy to walk her all the way to her doorstep, but he insisted. His mother raised him right. He was doing it for his mother, not for Molly.

"But I can see my house from here," Molly said at the intersection.

The neighbourhood was deserted, except for a couple of racoons watching them pass. The boy turned onto Molly's street despite her protests.

He is 'the boy' to me despite Molly telling me his name all the time. I don't want to know his name.

Anyway, they walked down the avenue lined with garbage cans and budding lilacs. The air smelled of summer even though it was only spring: soil moist from sprinklers, the boy's deodorant sharp and aggressive, lawnmower blades clogged with grass. Molly told him he smelled nice while she looked forward and walked, like a horse. She immediately regretted paying him the compliment and rubbed her hands together to keep either one from getting hold of him.

"Are you cold?" the boy asked.

"The grass smells nice," Molly said.

"No it doesn't," the boy said. "It smells like weed."

And then he started laughing, too loudly for a quiet street on a weeknight. Molly threaded her arm through his elbow and held onto him.

"Shh," she said placing her index finger across her pursed lips, such a cheesy gesture. They looked at each other: wet eyes, drunk complexions, stupid expressions.

"Look," the boy said and pointed to the dark pavement at their feet, "a BlackBerry." Molly followed his hand. Someone had left a fancy cell phone in the middle of the sidewalk, leather case and all.

***

Molly says I'm the only one who knows about the boy. I ask her: "What's there to know about?"

"You're the teacher," she says. "Aren't you supposed to lecture me about abuse of power?"

Molly says if she had to give me a conservative estimate of how often she thinks about him, it would be twenty-two times a day.

"Do you think about Mike, your husband?" I ask.

I say 'your husband' as if she doesn't know who Mike is to her. She tells me that the stupid boy dropped the BlackBerry they found down a sewer on his way home. She answers my ambivalent look with: "He was supposed to call the owner. Return it." And she laughs, twirls a strand of blonde hair and takes a sip of her latte. I remember how old the boy is, that he drinks beer, plays basketball at an idiotically expensive liberal arts college in the States. I know too much about him. Molly said he was always an arrogant prick in their sessions, except when he had a fresh injury and needed his mommy. She was glad when he was referred to another specialist. She tells me she's been having dreams about his mother lately and I change the subject and tell her about the production of *Hamlet* I saw at Stratford. But I can't even pay attention to myself because I keep thinking, *What does his mother have to do with anything?*

"We hugged at the end," Molly says.

***

I have become obsessed with morality. I read books I should have read in high school about the duality of human nature, the duplicity of man. I began with *Dr. Jekyll and Mr. Hyde, Hamlet,* and *Lolita.* I'm studying my own moral compass, which I've decided must be flawed. People tell me too much. Maybe it's the Polish thing? They see me as this Pope John Paul II, confessor of all their sins. I find myself being the keeper of friends' taboos: fantasies, secrets, queries. They fill me with their unmentionables, feel a bit better, and then I'm the one in need of catharsis, bogged down with shit. I've been writing short stories about it. I'm thinking about putting them into a collection that I could never publish, unless I want to live alone in some cave somewhere.

***

My partner Olivier has his kids this weekend. I bought $175-worth of groceries at No Frills and a case of Canadian. They wouldn't go for my usual Roncesvalles staples. Their mother baked a pie for our Victoria Day celebrations. It has a pastry top, so I can't tell what fruit is inside. It's hard to believe the little one, Andrew, was in grade one when Olivier and I first got together and now he has drinks with us on the balcony. The kids didn't know about me for a long time. Olivier and Dianne believe that children should be raised with a healthy attitude towards alcohol.

"You say you want me to drink around you," Andrew says after we refuse him a third beer. "I could just go drink behind a dumpster."

Olivier throws a can of Ginger Ale at him, which will explode moments later. We will all get sprayed a little but we'll laugh it off. The girl, Liz, is seventeen; she still comes over, too. She drinks the club soda and gin with extra lime wedges that I make for the two of us.

"I don't like beer either," she tells me and asks when Molly is coming over. It feels nice to be liked by teenagers.

Liz loves my friend Molly. Andrew calls her Smokin' Hot Sporty

Molly. Whenever the kids are over I make sure to organize some-thing with Molly: volleyball at Woodbine Beach; Frisbee on the is-land; a walk in Trinity Bellwoods. Molly brings Dr. Watson when we all walk to the park. Olivier takes his cell phone, which he checks often. His thumbs are always moving over it like he's mas-saging it, except when I ask: "Who are you texting?" and then he hides it and hugs me.

Molly is late. She arrives solo; her husband Mike is working. I like the word husband. He works constantly, which makes Molly act single. She is all dressed up: heels, skinny jeans, a backless halter-top. She's the only grown woman I know who can make trendy teen clothes look sexy and not cheap. We all crane our necks from the balcony and study Molly for a moment. She is tanned and shiny. It's hot out. She waves.

"No kebabs?" I ask. That was supposed to be her contribution to the barbecue.

"Pinot," she says and yanks a bottle of wine out of her purse by its neck.

I leave the others on the balcony and raise a finger at Liz who tries to follow me out into the living room. Just a sec. She looks at Molly when I do that.

Hugging Molly is something I look forward to, even though she's much smaller than me. She is soft yet firm, like an expensive mattress. A muscular back from all the rowing. When she hugs back she makes you feel wanted.

"I love you, Mol," I say. She kisses me on the cheek, looks truly amused, like I've just told her I'm pregnant.

"I love you too, babe," she says.

Molly and I met when I was gay. We were seventeen and my cousin Mike would buy us booze for house parties. Yes, the same Mike. Michał, really, but he's gone by Mike since high school. I warned Molly about marrying Mike. She warned me about messing around with a married man. Today, we could be mothers of seven-teen-year-olds, without scandal. Molly was supposed to go backpacking in Australia with me; she went to med school and married my cousin, Doctor Mike, instead. My mother is jealous her sister has a doctor for a son; she is of the mind that 'those who can't, teach.'

In the kitchen, which cannot be seen from our wraparound balcony, I take Molly's hand. She has a beautiful light pink manicure.

"Ooo, rich girl pink," I say. "I love it."

"You love everything, beer goggles," she says, fussing with her bra straps.

"Gin goggles," I say and stick my head into the fridge. "Drink?"

"I'm pregnant."

"Yeah, me too," I say and search the top shelf for club soda. "Everything works suddenly: my thyroid, my ovaries, the hormones—"

"—I'm serious."

I can't breathe. All I think of is the boy, the fucking BlackBerry.

Molly stands rigid in our kitchen. The iridescent backsplash Olivier installed glitters behind her sea-foam green top.

"You're serious," I say.

"Mike's thrilled," she says. "It's about time."

Liz comes into the kitchen.

"It *is* about time. I thought you'd never get here," she says and wraps her arms around Molly's waist from behind. Molly returns the embrace. I make myself another drink even though I feel inebriated.

***

She wants the boy to be desperately in love with her. The kind of love that makes him show up on her doorstep in the middle of the night after a frat-house bender, text her often, and attempt something.

"Like what?" I ask.

Molly's browsing through Craigslist for a crib.

"I keep hoping that he writes in his journal about me," she says.

Hope is the most metaphysically useless emotion: hope for everything, do nothing. And yet Molly is constantly doing. She baits the boy with emails, phone calls, presents.

"I sent him a book," she says, "for his birthday, last year."

"Did he read it?" I say. It's the closest I will come to criticizing my friend's behaviour, to her face. She's being so honest with me. Why can't I be honest with her? Shake her and tell her to get over it. To stop wasting her neurons on something she'd reject in an instant if it went her way.

"He told me the other day that our friendship means a lot to him."

I lower a mug of mint tea in front of typing Molly. Its rousing properties.

"You need to stop contacting him."

***

Olivier sent the kids to Québec to stay with his parents in Tadoussac for a month while he helps Dianne renovate the house. They're really too old to be *sent*. Andrew saw a Greenland shark there last summer, so he wanted to go back. Liz said she "needs" to finally have a beluga sighting, otherwise she won't believe they're there.

I've been to Dianne's house only once. Even though it's close, I don't like to go there. It reminds me of how bad I am at sharing. Of how possessive I can get of just thoughts, memories, history. Olivier is a masterful craftsman. He can do tiles, floors, cabinetry, like Bernini did his statues. But like Bernini, he can't choose the material as well as he can shape it. He'll work with whatever falls under his hands. So he says to me: "Slate or sea foam? Herringbone or checkerboard?"

"You want *me* to decide on Dianne's scheme?" I ask.

"I just need the final OK."

I study the samples, the fishy colours. Pick the opposite of everything in our apartment. I give her kitchen walls the colour of cigarette ash, but then I call Olivier and change it. I like Andrew and Liz. I don't want them to avoid the kitchen. I like Dianne too.

"Iceberg," I say into his voicemail. "2122-50, Benjamin Moore."

***

Olivier didn't come home last night. It's not completely unusual when he's out on a tight-deadline job, but the proximity of Dianne's house makes me worried. He could have stumbled home in the middle of the night. Unless something happened. I walk over. It's 7:45, warm and breezy. I drink a large black coffee on the way and listen to half of the new Arcade Fire CD I bought for myself as a summer vacation present. Teachers deserve presents.

The truck is in the driveway. Doorbell rings hollow. The jester-coloured stained glass in the front door makes everything inside distorted. I walk around the side of the house. A racoon-proofed garbage bin stands underneath the kitchen window. I'm light and coordinated enough to stand on top of it, peek inside.

"Pardon me?" a man's voice barks, startles me. I teeter on the bin and hang onto the brick wall. Miraculously, I don't fall, but scamper down like a drunken squirrel. "What *are* you doing?" an elderly man says. He's holding a hose. A soft weapon.

"I'm sorry," I say, brushing nothing off of my shorts. "I'm looking for the contractor. Olivier Brun? I'm his ... wife."

"Oh," the man says, pointing his hose at the ground instead of me, like he's disappointed that I am not an intruder. "You're the girlfriend." He waits.

"His partner," I say. I give him a reaction. The one he wants.

"His wife took him to emergency."

I don't hear what he says next because I am already jogging down to College Street to catch a cab. I go to Mount Sinai because that's where we went when I had the miscarriage. The old fart never said Dianne took Olivier to Mount Sinai.

The triage nurse and I have a brief spat about who I am and how I'm not supposed to be there, but then something happens and we click. Like when the zipper is stuck and you pull and tug and then it just shoots up because all you had to do was to align the two sides. I say my name and she shoots me a look of recognition and glances down at her nametag, her own first name full of consonants. She smiles and tells me the Bruns are on the seventh floor, in

Imaging. Why do I only now think of how strange it is that Dianne never changed her last name back? Olivier would say that's because Milosevic is a mouthful, and that he's been convicted of war crimes. And I would agree that it would be unfortunate to share a surname with a genocidal maniac.

***

They want to make sure it's not *Talk and Die*. That's what it's called when someone falls on his head and seems fine afterwards, and then dies of a haemorrhage to the brain several hours later. They say there is a clot in Olivier's brain, but only a small one. It can be melted away with medication. But it's good they checked it out. It's good they found out.

Dianne sits on a chair two feet away while I kiss Olivier on the head and whisper to him. She could slap my ass if she wanted to; she's so close. Olivier whispers back. Says he's sorry. I tell him anyone could fall, especially in his line of work.

The orderlies move him to another floor. Dianne and I leave Imaging together. In the mirrored elevator she says: "I'm glad at least that this happened while the kids are away." I can see all sides of her: tangles in the back of her hair, her severe profile, the slight curve of her back. "I want you to know I didn't intend for this."

It may be the caffeine or the adrenaline, but my hands are shaking like crazy. I stick them in my pockets. I'm suddenly hot all over, even though the place is air-conditioned like a morgue.

"Why?" I say. "Did you push him off the ladder?" A stupid chuckle.

There is a crooked smile across Dianne's face. She's quite a bit older than me, although you'd never know it. She looks at me with embarrassment, like she'd just congratulated me on a pregnancy while all I did was put on weight.

"He said he was going to tell you. Last week." She pulls a phone out of her purse.

We reach the ground floor. There are too many people, too many cash registers buzzing and clinking—bookstores, coffee shops, flowers, sandwiches, parking—to say: "Tell me what?"

"I have to get this," she says and motions with the phone. It's possible it could have rung.

GHOST

Andrew J. Borkowski

FOR TWO SUMMERS after my father's death, his ghost appeared at the top of the cottage stairs every night at twilight. You didn't see or hear him, you didn't sense any sudden chills. You smelled him. The unmistakeable pong of his body odour bit your nostrils just as you reached the landing and it permeated an air pocket about eight inches thick. You stepped into this pocket, caught a briny whiff of him, stepped back and it was gone. The scent was unmistakeable. A farm boy from the marshes of Polesie, dad never had much use for deodorant.

On the first evening he presented himself, my wife Therese was tucking in the kids in their bedroom just off the landing. Seeing the look on my face, she silently mouthed the words: "Do you smell that?"

The next evening, it was there again. The same place, the same time, as we were putting the girls to bed. We had cleared out all of Dad's things months earlier, but Therese and I searched drawers and closets downstairs for some scrap of bedding or clothing that might be the culprit. We found nothing.

"It's the kids," Therese said. "He's come to say goodbye to his grandchildren."

The day my father was struck by a car in front of St. Voytek's church on Copernicus Avenue, Therese and I and my brother Blaise made it to his bedside before the intensive care staff shut down his life support. We had left our daughters with a neighbour. Now, we convinced ourselves, he was coming back to complete this unfinished business.

It made sense that he would choose the cottage to do it. Dad bought the place, near Kendal on Lake Simcoe, in the autumn of 1960, one of the shambling clapboard places built by British-born emigrés trying to replicate the feeling of English country villages, giving the shore the atmosphere of a place longing to be somewhere else, settings for high teas and croquet.

Got Junk

I spend my afternoons emptying out the "old building," the stub of the original cottage we left standing when we built the dream home Dad planned to retire to. In the old dining room, the lattice windows show daylight around their sills as I arrange the items we plan to sell in a yard sale. Most of the antique furniture from the original cottage was ruined by rain during construction of the new building. Smaller pieces have fallen victim to the animals we've been unable to keep out since my father's death: raccoons, birds, (including a duck which fell down the chimney during a fall migration), and squirrels who covered the kitchen in pasty excrement after devouring the box of All Bran that Dad had left out on his last visit.

I'm hoping that the sale of what's left will pay for the dumpster for GOTJUNK.COM that sits on the back lawn, a receptacle for the useless material that my father hoarded in crawlspaces and sheds. My skin burning with the solvents I apply to dissolve the clots of rust that hold it together, I dismember the swing set I erected years ago for my girls, when I hoped the cottage would be for them the sanctuary that it had been for me. The dumpster tolls out my failure to provide that with each section I toss into its empty hull.

Difficult Places: Earth

Dad's vegetable patch stands a few yards beyond the dumpster, a bed ten by twenty feet framed in four-by-fours that once held up the porch roof of the old cottage. Stakes that supported tomatoes, runner beans, and raspberries have been scribbled over with deadly nightshade and strangling dog vine. Two bone-white sticks, lashed together with rags, shape a sloppy crucifix at the edge of the bed, marking the final task that awaits me.

A few defiant sunflowers, stubborn as the man who planted them, penetrate a chicken wire roof built as a futile barrier against rabbits. Neither the war, nor thirty years of crunching numbers at the Parish Trust could kill Dad's attachment to the soil. We have a picture of him waist deep in barley, felling great swathes of it with a scythe. The handfuls of dwarf cucumbers and sparse tomatoes this garden yielded were place-holders, stand-ins for the beets and potatoes his family had clawed out of the Pripet marshes until the SS put an end to them in 1942. This place was home to a different man from the one we knew in the city, a contingent self to whom war had not happened, who never came to Canada to take up a desk job and become our father.

The cottage garden wasn't the ideal place to reclaim the land. Its dense clay soil crushed roots and stunted tubers. Topsoil had to be carried in sacks or hauled by wheelbarrow from the road. Water had to be carried up from the lake, bucket by bucket. To a man like Dad, a thing wasn't worth doing unless it was done in the most difficult way possible. Why replace a water pump when the original, which looked like a relic salvaged from the *Lusitania*, could be patched into sclerotic life with putty and coat hangers? Why buy cordwood when, for the price of a bottle or two of Żubrówka, a local farmer would let you harvest a stand of maples with a borrowed chain saw and you could spend whole summers splitting logs by hand? Work was his fitness regime; he'd snort at joggers on the shore road and demand: "Where are they running? Why don't they chop wood? That is *real* exercise."

Difficult Places: Water

Mid-afternoon. The sun blazing overhead. Dad would never have acknowledged a day like this as too hot to work when there were hedges to trim, lawns to cut, or dumpsters to fill, but I pour a beer into a glass and trudge down to the water. All that remains of the trifurcated willow that shaded the leisurely afternoons of our youth is a single trunk that now leans out over the breakwater, its tresses straining for the surface, yearning to fall.

Afternoons we'd sit strumming our guitars in the willow's shade, high on something if my brother Blaise was there, and Dad would come down with a glass of beer, wearing the same ragged work pants that I'm wearing now, hitched at the waist with a safety pin. I have not inherited his rail thin cavalryman's physique. At my age, Dad still had a waistline and clothes hung carelessly on his frame. I've got the physiognomy of stocky uncles whom I have only seen stiffly posed in prewar photos and my midsection pushes out in lobes over the waistband of his old trousers. I crouch in the spindle of shade that the willow still manages to cast and take solace in the lake: the one thing that we thought would never change.

If heaven is eternity in the place you've been most at peace, mine will be here, reliving that first immersion after a Friday night drive up from town, the cool water slaking the itch of the city on my skin, wreathed in the slippery bodies of my children. I've seen this water sundazzled and playful as quicksilver under a midday sun, as a wavering column that tethered me to the moon. I've seen its dock-destroying rage as storms pushed their bruised faces across it, trailing black locks of rain. I've stretched out on its skin at midnight and felt myself sucked up into a dizziness of stars. But the stars have been disappearing as the city metastasizes northward.

"They are building, they are building, they are building," Dad said as subdivisions advanced like panzer battalions along the ridge behind us, "but they will never build on top of that water!"

He didn't anticipate that what "they" couldn't build on they would poison.

A watery holocaust is in progress. A yellow fin breaks the surface, flutters and sinks, then another and another. Dad didn't fish, so the deepwater pike, pickerel, and muskie that lived in Simcoe's reedy deeps were rumours to us as kids. The odd one struggled into these shallows to die. Now, the lake's massive bottom-feeding carp are dying in the thousands. They've caught a virus brought through the Trent canal system in the bilges of houseboats. It's the latest in a string of plagues since my father's death: algae blooms, zebra mussels, and infestations of E. coli.

The summer my father's fragrant ghost appeared at the top of the stairs, we vowed to keep the cottage, but the strain of living in two places, the recession, and the pressures of a two-career family made it impossible. We began to argue about the place, as I remembered my parents arguing. My girls have never summered here and, the one year Therese and I managed to coordinate a vacation, police boats trolled for the body of a man who'd drowned the weekend before, while an E. coli outbreak kept us off the beaches further north.

Now it's the carp. Limpet mines of decaying fish flesh bob shoreward to collect and stink in nooks along the shore, omens of a dead dream.

Neighbour Doug

"How're you, folks?"

Doug Peavers stands at the top of the bank, one gauntleted fist cocked on his hip, the other clutching a trident, a cross between Neptune and Hephaestus in hip waders, a twin-chambered gas mask at his chin.

Doug is the self-appointed kapo of the neighbourhood campaign against the carp. He's drafted his kids and their friends, kitted them in rubber and armed them with pitchforks. All week long, they've been forking dead fish out of the lake and depositing them in garbage bags along the shore.

"They gots herpes," he explains. "Some kinda a fish herpes. Killed millions of 'em in Scugog last year."

Neighbour Doug knows all about the koi herpes virus that's killing the carp, and he describes the sunken eyes, bleeding gills and blistered skins on their corpses in loving detail. He's an expert on the constitutional status of dead fish: the province is responsible for the water, the feds own the shore, and the township owns the road. The town will only collect the corpses if they're dragged across jurisdictional lines onto its turf and deposited in green garbage bags on the gravel shoulder.

"So me and the kids, we're takin' charge, like. We pulled up three hundred since Monday. Got any garbage bags?"

Doug would really like a beer. We are meant to have a bond, because our families have been neighbours for fifty years and Doug is the last surviving denizen of Morris Meadows, a collection of ramshackle cottages that used to flank us to the south. The Meadows families weren't like us. The women all smoked Players' Plain, drank beer from stubbies, and said "Fuck" a lot. Their Saturday night corn roasts took place over the back hedge, a column of sparks from their fire wavering over the cedars in time to choruses of "Roll me Over In the Clover." On Sunday mornings, Dad exacted his revenge by burning yard waste, smoking the Meadows crowd out of their sleep-ins and unleashing the fury of their hangovers.

That miserable summer I stayed up to help Dad and his Polish friends build the new cottage, Doug and I became friends, bombing around the back roads in his family's station wagon swigging Molson's and listening to "Flying Purple People Eater" on an eight-track called *Goofy Greats*. Dad countered my rebellion with stone-faced stoicism.

In the old building, I take a beer from the Shelvador refrigerator which still works, if loudly, seventy-five years after it rolled off the line in Galt, Ontario. Doug opens it with his teeth, spits out the cap, and studies the fridge's art deco moulding.

"You could get good money for that fridge. Guys are buyin' em, paintin' em and stickin' beer kegs inside."

After Morris sold off the Meadow cottages to his tenants, Doug inherited his father's shack and moved in. He's at home in Kendal: plays hockey and ice fishes by winter, cruises the lake with his family by summer in the Starcraft Deckboat he keeps moored to a landing he bought from DockinaBox in Barrie. He takes his kids to Santa's Village in Bracebridge. We don't do any of these things. We talk to each other across a divide. I haven't told him I'm selling, but he knows. He's seen the real estate agents coming and going, heard the dumpster toll as I jettison my patrimony. And he knows I know it's him who's put the word out, prompting a steady stream of discreet and not-so-discreet inquiries from local tradesmen hoping we'll panic and opt for a private sale as prices stall and the recession begins to bite.

I contribute a box of garbage bags to Doug's war against the carp. He tells me there'll always be a room at his house whenever Therese and I want to come visit. We both know that won't happen.

The Spectre

I trudge upstairs to the bathroom and stop on the landing, as has become my reflex since we first scented him that summer, and I rock back and forth across his pocket in the air. Two steps forward, two steps back. Every night he'd return to the same place at the same time. I'd hold my hand to the edge of his envelope, push my nose past it, smelling him, then not smelling him; then draw back, smelling him, not smelling him. After the girls got boyfriends and summer jobs, the odour began to fade. As the apparitions became more intermittent, my rocking and sniffing became more compulsive.

Seaplane Man

I take a trowel and probe around the makeshift crucifix in the vegetable patch, parting the dog vine to break a scorched crust of dandelion and plantain, when Tom Laidlaw appears with gifts of corn, carrots, and peas from his own garden. Our neighbour to the north, Lord of the Shore, Tom has been coming here since the days when the drive from Toronto took all day and a trolley from Newmarket ran along the town line behind our properties.

As kids, we knew him as the Seaplane Man. On summer evenings, we'd rush to the beach to watch him touch down in his Cessna floatplane while our own father crawled up from the city in a used car redolent with bagels and kielbasa from Copernicus Avenue delis. Our mother would admire his languid, jaunty motions as he leapt from the cabin to the dock and secured the plane, an apparition from the world of television: a Sky King in white loafers, lemon yellow polo shirts, and glinting Ray-Bans. And we'd think: "That's what dads are supposed to be like."

Tom sets the bags of vegetables at my feet and surveys the sad patch that dad's garden has become through shades that mask the glaucoma that has forced him to give up flying.

"Just tidying up," I say.

The Seaplane Man nods vaguely. "Whoever buys this place will probably just build over this patch."

Which is precisely why I need to dig here, but I don't tell him that.

"I miss your Dad, you know. He was a fine man. That generation. The war. We owe those guys more than we can ever repay."

I look down at the paint-spattered toecaps of my father's work boots while Tom searches for a trace of my father in me. Dad and the Seaplane Man were friends, sharing a wifeless devotion to the Shore long after both their spouses declared their dislike for the place and stopped coming. Dad promised him that, should he ever sell, he'd approach Tom first. I've tried to honour that promise, but the price of oil has bankrupted Tom's Middle Eastern clients, making my failure his. The vegetables are his atonement. I murmur my thanks, but when I look up the Seaplane Man has flown.

Buyers

Rick the Roofer claims to be a friend of Doug Peavers. He lives a quarter mile up the shore and talks as if we'd known each other for centuries, spicing his conversation with tales of misadventures in the taverns of Kendal. The day Rick presents his offer, he arrives with two buddies, a brother-in-law who claims to be a building inspector and a guy who says he knows wiring. His accomplices amble through the house, pulling on bottles of Labatt's 50, shaking heads at the electrical panel, the fireplace, and the wood-burning stoves. "It's not tuh code, Rick," they mumble. "Yuh'll have to rip that out ... the insurance'll never stand for it ... that's a fire trap."

Rick studies me over the lip of his beer, gauges the impact of his friends' performance, then studies the offer sheet curled in his hand.

"Jeez, guys. I dunno. Alex here and me, I think we both thought we had a deal. Aw, what the fuck."

He shrugs and hands me the offer. It's a hundred thousand less than my asking.

I drop my price by twenty thousand. Rick's accomplices scoff.

"C'mon, Alex. It's gonna cost me at least two hundred thou just to get this place to a state where someone'll insure it."

The henchmen slap down their beers on the kitchen table. "Don't do this, Rick. I'm tellin' ya."

The three of them force me back against the kitchen counter. A gust through the kitchen window laces their beery breath with the pong of rotting carp. I'm still a city boy; they're the ones who belong here. Tonight they'll be in the bar at the Shore Inn, bragging how they swindled the Polack's faggot son. I'm overcome by the need to be done with this place. We settle for forty below asking.

After they've left, I rock myself in the once-haunted slice of air on the landing. Two steps forward, two steps back. All I smell is beer and dust and fish.

"I'm sorry, Dad," I whisper. "I'm sorry."

Burial at Sea

I go back to the garden, uproot the crucifix and lay it gently on the grass. This time I use a spade to cut down to where his final third should be. Blaise took a third of him back to Poland. Another third is buried in Weston. I have to fill a whole bucket to be sure I have all of him.

I've had this gesture planned from the moment we decided to sell, pictured myself scattering his ashes in wisps over sun-dappled water. But it's choppy today and the waves lunge for him as I wade in. By the time I'm out far enough for the current to take him, I'm struggling with a bucket of mud. I manage to dispense a few hand-fuls, until the bucket slips from my hand sending up a cloud of blue murk. I stand waist deep in him, batting away carp corpses with my trowel, until he settles.

Walk

On our last evening, Therese and I walk the shore road as I've done for as many summers as I can remember. A few of the old gable-and-clapboard cottages still stand, each one showing a light in its mys-terious heart. As boys, my brother and I would go "sneaking" along this road at night. Defying larger-than-life NO TRESPASSING signs, we'd challenge ourselves to negotiate the shore without touching pavement. We'd keep ourselves hidden from view, threading our way through the prickly interiors of the hedgerows, skirting falls of mossy rock and the ruins of the jazz age dance hall that had burned down the summer before my father bought the place. It was as if we were applying the lesson we'd learned watching him haul his water, chop his wood, trim his cedars in the dark: the more difficult a job could be made, the higher its moral reward.

A wind comes up in the night and I wake to the rustle of trees that are no longer there, to the snap of flags that no longer fly. Dad kept the cottage long after he realized he'd never retire here. His being here was a gesture in a world where gestures were all that was left of what he had left behind. He'd been forced to let go once. He wasn't going to let go again. I've had to do that for him, put the alternate Dad who dwelt here to rest. But what about my own con-tingent selves? I get up and walk empty rooms where my mother is happy and knitting by the fire, where I write the poems I never wrote, where I still sleep with the girls I dreamed of bringing here in secret. Out in the promising dark, the dead presidents I thought I'd be play croquet and touch football on the lawn, spies and explorers pick their difficult way along the shore, astronauts vault at the moon, and my brother and I sit stoned and strumming under the willow. What will happen when all these shades have been set free? Where will I leave my scent?

BOTTLENECK

Ania Szado

NADA REMEMBERS CARRYING her father's beer bottles out of the living room, when she was nine and ten and eleven, by crooking her fingers in their mouths. She liked the smoothness of the glass throats against her knuckles and fingertips. She liked the weight. The bottles stank of the cigarette butts her dad dropped into the empties as he wept into the night. She smelled her fingers every morning as she walked to school, sniffing the stink of stale tobacco and beer.

The memory comes to her as she holds Arlo's erection in her hand. Its opening yawns, a small pink mouth begging for the tip of her tongue.

Erection: that's how she always thinks of Arlo's thing. The word *penis* sounds medical, and he got rattled when she once called it a cock. His erection isn't what she would call a cock anyway. Cocks are meaty and dark—the wide barrel of a stubby, the squat Canadian beer bottle that is now a thing of the past. Arlo's is slender and fine like the neck of a modern tall-boy bottle. Nice enough, and does a good job too, but far too elegant for the bluntness of *cock*.

Arlo has no hair around his penis. No hair on his balls. Nada clutches and rubs. She reminds herself to stop thinking in the negative. It isn't that her fiancé has no pubic hair, it's that he is hairless. See? Anything can be framed without the use of the word *no*, if you try hard enough. And she is trying. She is trying very hard. She's determined to eradicate her negativity before the wedding.

How many weeks until the big day? She closes her mouth over Arlo's erection and counts silently as she bobs.

She met him in April, in a bar. He had been leaning against the wall in a huddle of handsome guys wearing leather jackets. Nada was at a small table with her friend Rosanne.

Rosanne pointed with her bottle. She said: "Check it, Nad—them dudes. Wow."

Nada said: "I hate guys who travel in packs."

"Of course you do."

"They're just propping up each other's egos."

"You're fucking crusty."

"And you're in a shitty mood."

"Am now," Rosanne said.

Nada wasn't crusty; she was incisive and direct, a no-bullshitter —people appreciated that. Or they used to. The loving seemed to be getting thin as Nada squeaked toward her twenty-fifth birthday. That morning, a co-worker had called her cranky. What a word; it made Nada's lip curl. Cranky, like a whiny child.

And then, on a lunchtime call, a headhunter told her she had a reputation for being flinty. Flint was sharp. It implied precision, control. But Nada's "That's good, right?" was met with awkward silence.

Now Rosanne had clammed up, too.

Nada said: "Everyone's in a foul mood these days."

Rosanne said: "Someone's a big black hole that sucks everyone in."

Nada went to the restroom. When she came out, only one leather jacket dude was still warming the wall. He had slid down halfway into a sloppy squat. He looked up at her, up her legs, up her skirt.

"Hi," she said.

He grinned. "Truth. I am indeed high."

"And also, you are low."

He laughed, and almost tipped over.

Nada reached out to steady him. He pulled himself up to standing.

"That, too," he said.

"What?"

"You said, 'You are low.' That's my name: Arlo. What's yours?"

"Nada."

"Nada as in 'nothing'? Like you're a negative? I've been rescued by a ghost-girl! By the power of your powers, you grant me: nothing!" He grabbed her arm as she turned away. "It's the perfect name for you."

"Sure," she said. "Like 'Lo' is perfect for you." He belonged on the floor. She was itching to knock him down there herself.

Arlo said: "We need to toast our mutual excellence. I'll buy you a drink. There's nothing like 'nothing.' Nada is beautiful! Nothing is ... perfection."

In spite of herself, she smiled. What a clown.

She pulls away as Arlo's erection begins to spew. She shouldn't think of clowns during sex. If she starts associating clowns with his candlestick shaft and smiling pink penis-head, she'll never make it to the wedding.

"Nada," he gasps, "you're a goddess."

Twenty-eight weeks until the ring goes on.

Next week, she'll blow him in twenty-seven slurpy thrusts. The week after, twenty-six. By the time they get to the honeymoon, she'll only have to look at him and lick her lips, and he'll come.

***

Thinking positive is harder at work. The culture is all rah-rah and give-a-hundred-and-ten-percent, but the team is used to relying on Nada for one sane dissenting voice. It has served them well. Not that shaping their clients' brands is rocket science, but ....

Nada stops, does a self-check. Too negative? She adjusts: Shaping clients' brands is easy. Or at least, it is for her. It comes naturally to her. So much so that she feels confident declaiming when the enthusiastic ideas being pitched by the boss or the clients themselves are off-track. So much so that even Jeremy, the boss of all, listens when Nada says no.

But now she can't say or think *no*. And after the third squirming meeting in which she has hemmed and hedged, searching for ways to put her thoughts in a sunny light, she can already feel her influence and respect slipping away.

Damn it, she thinks. What's wrong with *no*, anyway?

What is wrong is that it's her name. Nada. Nothing. Negative, negative, negative. Why should she have to toe the line that was written on her birth certificate? A name isn't fate. It isn't immutable.

She has tried to bend it, now and again, over the years. But somehow it always sways back to the same equilibrium, and once again she finds herself accused of being pessimistic. Always the cynic. Always with the *no*.

She has had it with bending. This time, she's breaking it. She is going to start a new life with a new attitude, with new words, a new response. Yes. Always yes. Everything good. She would make it good.

She would make it.

Twenty weeks.

***

Her birth certificate says Nada, but her father's sister called her Nadzia. Aunt Truda had come from the Old Country to help care for Nada when she was born. There were three things Truda did daily: work the early shift cleaning the seniors' home on Sherman Avenue, cook dinner, and sleep. There were two things she did at least once a week: bathe, and snipe about Nada's name. She thought it moronic that her niece was called Nada, instead of the fine Polish name, Nadzia. She took it as a personal affront that Nada didn't correct her teacher during roll call every day.

Nada's classrooms were full of Italian, Polish, and Irish surnames. The latter came with good first names, too: Nancy, John, Karen. The others morphed swiftly from Pasquale to Pat, Philomena to Philly, Bozena to Barb.

In grade 3, Nada pulled a younger student aside. Aggie's accent was thick as sour cream. "What's your real name?"

The girl's cheeks turned pink. "Agnieszka." Tears trembled along her lashes. "Don't tell."

Aggie thought maybe Nada was meant to be Nadzia all along,

that some civil servant might have dropped the ZI as he typed up the birth registration. That's what Aggie said had happened to her brother Alex, who nevertheless endured being called "Aleksy," his intended name, at home.

When Nada shared the story of Alex-Aleksy with her aunt, Truda shooed it away as though urging chickens back to the barn. "If your mother had lived, you would have been Nadzia on paper and in every mouth. No man behind a counter would have dared change such a beautiful name. You are Nada because your idiot father called you that; that's all. With your mother dead so fast, without even the chance to hold her baby, your father had nothing. And so!"

Nada had frowned, uncomprehending.

Truda said: "Nada means 'nothing'—don't you know?" She slid two plates of scrambled eggs and potatoes onto the kitchen table and sat down heavily.

Nada felt like she was going to be sick.

Her aunt slammed her fork down. "Don't start with your moping, Nadzia! It's not like you meant to kill your mother. Let me see you make the sign of the cross. Now thank the Lord that your mama held on long enough to give birth. And thank His Blessed Mother that I came over to raise you. And when you're done with that, you might think about thanking me."

Truda hauled herself out of the chrome chair, went to the cupboard, and returned with two miniature bottles. Bright white Pop Shoppe logos gleamed against the backdrop of crimson cream soda. "This will put the colour back in your cheeks. Red things are very good for you. Tomorrow I'll make beets."

***

Nada had revelled in her name briefly—during her high school punk rock years. Her boyfriend and his friends went by Viper, Snot, and X-it, but only she had nihilism stamped and sealed into her official ID. Not that her ID got much use in those days. She slipped into bars as Laura Prendergast or Julie Little—whichever older girl-friend could spare her photo identity card on any given night, granting Nada an alcoholic glow that led, inevitably, to a sloppy basement screw.

It's been a while since she thought of Viper or his Pop Shoppe mini-bottle cock. Not that she had used the C-word with him. She tried calling it a *rod* once, but Viper said: "Rod is my dad's name, you stupid bitch." And then she was left with nothing. It always came down to that.

***

It's twelve weeks to the wedding, and Nada has lost her appetite. At home, she lubes surreptitiously before joining Arlo in bed. She's down to a dozen head-bobs now, but she knows the intricacies of her fiancé's wand like she knows the peaks of her ever-sharpening cheekbones; she rebalances the distribution of hand job to blowjob, and she doesn't disappoint.

At work, her teammates drift around her as though they, and not she, are the ghosts.

On Thursday, her reflection in the Butcher Delight window startles her. Her eyes have gotten so large. She likes that. But she's forced now to consider her jutting hipbones. This won't do. The dress won't fit. It was her mother's dress, made to measure in War-saw, and there's no way Nada is going to cut it down.

She buys three steaks, goes home, and pan-fries one. She eats quickly, pausing for salt but not for breath. When Arlo arrives she broils the remaining two, pours them each a large glass of wine, and chews slowly.

"Look at you savouring that," he says, his smile as lascivious as it gets. "You do like your meat, don't you?"

On Friday she wears a short skirt to a meeting and sits well back from the boardroom table, her knees pressed together and her hem two inches from her crotch. Everyone who enters the room stares at the gap between her thighs. Jeremy can't tear his eyes away. People love negative space, Nada thinks, and for the first time in a while, she laughs. The meeting goes uphill from there. She's back in her skin, if not in her naturally sceptical mind. She makes a steeple of her fingers, moving her thumbs low to create a vaginal shape. She concentrates on listening with her lips parted. The room feels electric; she could make the air crackle if she rubbed her nylons together. She licks her lips. They're dry, but inside her skirt, she's getting moist.

She stops to buy ground beef on the way home and finds herself transfixed by the bison burgers. Why can't she be marrying a cowboy, instead of a division manager of an online greeting card company? A cowboy named ...

She mulls it over. Cliff. Cliff with low-heeled roper boots and rough, awkward hands—hands that would hesitate on her blouse but could flip and tie a calf as quick and clean as she herself could ply a silk scarf. Imagine those calloused fingers fumbling with her tiny iridescent buttons. How the bulge in his jeans would echo the rising exasperation in his eyes. She can almost taste the word *cock* in her mouth. Hunger shoots through her. She grabs a box of bison burgers and hurries for home.

Arlo needs a nickname. She needs a nickname. She can't last another almost-three-months as Nada Narowski. She floats the idea over Scrabble. "You be Warlock. Your real name is right inside it. I'll be Naro."

She trades in a tile. Arlo adds ES to the word *stitch*.

He says: "Naro sounds like 'narrow,' and you're already too thin."

"So make it Nar, then. N-A-R."

"Not G-N-A-R?"

"I don't want a silent letter," she says—but in her mind, she is suddenly, secretly Gnar with a G—a little snarly, a little scary, and not afraid to bare her teeth.

The sex that night is wild-buffalo-wild. Gnar forgets she's too skinny. Warlock's erection turns magically robust. She mounts him after twelve. He doesn't pull out to ejaculate, as per their usual agreement. That was between Nada and Arlo. Nada and Arlo are gone.

***

Nine weeks to go and Nada and Arlo are fully back.

***

Four weeks, and Nada fills out her wedding dress to perfection.

"Well, as close as it gets," says the seamstress doing the fine adjustments. "Nothing is perfect, right?"

***

Two weeks before the wedding, the girlfriends throw Nada a spectacularly drunken party at the bar where she and Arlo met. The theme is drink. The games are drinks. The dinner is drinks. The decorations are drinks. They drink the drinks, the decorations, the gifts. Nada drinks enough to vomit in the car, on her front porch, and in the shoes her friend Stacy has just removed from Nada's feet.

"I'm sorry," Nada wails. She wonders when she started sobbing. Maybe she has been sobbing all night.

"Forget it," Stacy says. "Just don't wake up dead."

The afternoon is old by the time Nada wakes. She takes a sip of water and pukes painfully. Her throat hurts. Her tongue looks carpet-burned. She has a slight recollection of the party moving, on staggering foot, from the threshold of the bar to someone's apartment above a nearby store. Who does she know that lives over a store? Not a soul. Nobody. She shuts her eyes against the pain in her skull, and tries to concentrate.

Maybe if she puts it positively.

Someone she met last night lives above a store near the bar, and Nada and her girlfriends fucked him and his friends last night.

Her eyes crack open and she heaves into the toilet. She washes up and moves slowly back to bed, the skin of her queasy stomach sagging in her hands.

***

A week to go. Her dad phones. "You don't tell your father you're getting married? You don't send him an invitation?"

"You won't be missing much," she says.

"That makes me sad, Nada."

"Think of it this way, then. You'll have more fun at home."

"You don't want me there?"

"I *do* want you to know I'll be thinking of you." She's getting good at this positive reframing business. "It's a tiny guest list, Dad. Just a few friends."

"If you don't have family at your wedding, you aren't legally married."

She laughs weakly, taken aback by her relief at the possibility of an out.

***

Small wedding, small wedding party, small chapel, but the guest book the chaplain brings out is big and ornate.

"This is the exciting part," he says. "The first time signing your married name."

Nada's signature on the license was a hurried scrawl, but now she feels like Princess Diana hovering her pen above the line. When she orders her new ID, she'll be going all the way: first name, middle name, last. What she writes on this gilded page will be her identity from here on.

She has played with a hundred possibilities. She has scoured the thesaurus for opposites of the word *nothing*. Her attitude and her vocabulary have been scrubbed of all things negative.

This is it: the new life. The life of "I do."

The reception dinner is subdued. She smiles and kisses the half-dozen guests, but only Arlo seems genuinely happy. He pulls her close, grinning, and growls into her ear: "I'll be your Warlock tonight, Nar. I can't wait."

But she's not a Nar or Narowski anymore. She's a Miller. Susan Amanda Miller. She kisses Arlo chastely, as a Susan Miller would.

***

She phones her father from the cab on the way to the hotel.

He says: "So my Nada is a wife now. I wish you the best."

"Thank you. But I'm not Nada anymore. I'm changing everything, my entire name."

There's a pause. Then her father says: "I gave you this name, Nada." His voice falters. "I gave you this name because of what it means. It means 'Hope'."

Nada listens closely; her father has begun to cry. She hears the unmistakable sound of a beer cap being twisted off.

It's Arlo, beside her in the taxi. He has smuggled a Coors Lite from the reception.

"To Susan," he says. He lifts it by its long glass neck.

A TEMPORARY PINPRICK

Anna Mioduchowska

IT WAS ALMOST closing time at the Hudson's Bay when Ziutka stood in front of the store's book section and considered stealing a book. Her spruce green winter coat, made especially for the move to Canada, weighed heavily on her shoulders just now. It was lined with the sheared sheepskin vest she had brought out of Warsaw, along with her two-month-old son, from the Uprising almost twenty years ago. Made of good quality worsted wool, the coat was ideal for daily bus stop vigils. The bribe she had slipped the salesclerk to put the fabric away for her had been worth it; Canadian winters were everything her sister had promised. Unfortunately, the store was overheated—all stores were overheated—which seemed to Ziutka an awful waste, not to mention a cause of discomfort. Ziutka wished there was a chair, or bench nearby.

Why So Tired? read the bold black print on the front cover of the book displayed on the top shelf, and Ziutka responded by becoming even more conscious of the fatigue accumulated in her fifty-six-year-old body. The softer, lighter hue of *What You Can Do About It*, running across the lower half of the cover heightened the effect. Why is it always up to me, a voice inside her whined even as its rational, self-disciplined counterpart shushed it so she could concentrate. Ziutka stared at the letters until they began to shift and reassemble themselves to form a hand reaching out to her. The hand held a gift of understanding and a promise of remedy, and was as hard to resist as a sweet poppy seed bun for a five-year-old. Every penny in the budget was spoken for, and the supply of the little blue pills the doctor continued to prescribe to her was running low. The neighbourhood pharmacist, who spoke Ukrainian, a language she thought she had left behind with childhood, and which was slowly returning now to fill the communication void, had warned her of the drug's dangerous side-effects. The pills were the only thing that stood between her and the insomnia-induced visions of herself as an ant cruel children had buried under a large mound of dirt. She had to have the book even if it meant stealing it.

The *how* was not a problem. In comparison to the most straight-forward assignment during her years in the Underground, or obtaining the simplest everyday objects in the years after the war and occupation, this was child's play. The moral justification? Ziutka had never stolen anything before, yet the idea of simply taking the book had slipped into her mind so effortlessly she barely had time to take another breath before all the explanations for the theft lined up for inspection.

"The two younger children are still in school, Your Honour, the third one struggling," she addressed the imaginary judge. "My husband is on the verge of a breakdown, and the pay I bring home every two weeks would be a good joke if I didn't spend so many hours shackled to the sewing machine to earn it—overtime pays time and a half, Your Honour. If Janek becomes sick we will be reduced to begging, and I've no experience with that."

Would the world be a worse place if she stole the book? This book would save her, and along with her, the rest of the family. Of that she had no doubt, just as she had no doubt that her life was a series of ill-fitting chapters, written by a perverse author who made sure that at the beginning of each chapter she once again started from zero, ignorant as ever of the author's intentions and forced to improvise. Except that improvisation suggested a pre-existing theme. What if she were caught? This was not the nineteenth century; no one was going to put her away for the rest of her life for this crime, although the prospect of stability, her own cell, and time on her hands, did not sound unappealing just now. Ziutka gazed at the books in front of her with the same longing that had gripped her the first summer in Edmonton three years ago whenever she saw someone licking an ice cream cone. One cone cost only twenty five cents, but twenty five cents times five people made a dollar twenty five. Walking home from the bus one day Ziutka had found a dime. Treating herself to ice cream with coins the universe had chosen to drop at her feet was not taking away from her family. She walked with her eyes glued to the ground for days afterward.

Viewed from the perspective of her need, and of the crimes she had witnessed which had gone unpunished, theft of one book would make a hole no larger than a pinprick in the world's moral fibre. A temporary pinprick. "When I get home, Your Honour, I'll make a dust jacket to protect the cover, and bring the book back as soon as I've finished reading it." It would take a while of course. In spite of the weekly lessons with Mrs. Dunn, her English was still in the diaper stage. With the help of the children, and the dictionary which was beginning to resemble an old woman's prayer book, she should be able to manage it. Once her fatigue was under control, she should be able to manage anything.

One fluid gesture, natural and invisible as smoothing one's hair on a windy day, and the book was under Ziutka's arm. She walked purposely to the Jasper Avenue exit, raised the collar of her coat and put on her gloves, then pushed the heavy door and walked out with the dignity befitting a woman her age. A closer inspection, if any-one cared to look, would reveal that she was biting her lower lip, as if to suppress a sudden urge to laugh. "Stolen book found on a woman arrested on the charge of disturbing the peace with uncon-trolled mirth." The urge was an old friend. At fifteen, she had laughed while crossing the river Zbrucz, which at that time separ-ated Russia and Poland, because the rotund woman in front of her had made such a loud splash entering the water. After a night spent creeping through the forest behind the smugglers, all but holding her breath, this was the proverbial straw on a camel's back. She con-tinued to laugh as Polish border guards ordered the four in her group to raise their arms once they reached the other shore, and march to the wooden house that served as headquarters. She burst out laughing during a state funeral mass when an outraged voice behind her whispered that she should take off her student cap. *"Boys today have no manners."* She had to struggle to keep a straight face all through her own marriage ceremony in 1942, which took place only because their priest pleaded so passionately with the bishop to permit the use of their Underground pseudonyms on the marriage certificate.

The sidewalk was crowded with Thursday night shoppers, mostly women who worked during the day, brown paper shopping bags brushing against their legs. Conscious of the late hour they hurried to catch a bus or find their car; it would be almost bed-time by the time they got home, and there were still lunches to be made, clothes prepared for morning and tomorrow's dinner started. Snowflakes in less of a hurry to reach their destination settled on hair, noses. By morning, the city would wake up looking as fresh as the soul of a sinner after confession. Protective of the stolen book, Ziutka stood for a moment surveying the scene before her as if from a great distance, then slipped it into her bag, pulled back her shoulders, turned left, and marched toward the bus stop on the corner of 101st and Jasper. This would make a good story, she thought later inside the crowded bus, too bad she couldn't tell it to anyone. She immediately reprimanded herself. What she had just done was not praiseworthy. It was simply necessary.

TOSIA

Christijan Robert Broerse

Chowamy w sercu.
(We hide in our heart)
—Grażyna Chrostowska

And There It is again, hovering in the air like dusk falling hard upon wooden floorboards. It is there, too, on the ornate curves of carved banisters of this ancient East German apartment building where I now live.

It seems improbable, even impossible that this tender and aromatic revelation should be waiting for me here in this particular place. Daniella's door closes behind me with a hard click; she is teaching me German, but suddenly the world changes and there is a new sense of loss in my thoughts. I breathe deeply, going down the first set of steps.

In these old buildings, you feel each crack in the wood, each tread of tenants past and present as if the stairs were also built to tell tales, proclaiming their mundane comings and goings.

But now that smell of perfume hangs in the air; it is there, boastful in the dark sheen of the wood, in the grey clouds floating outside the window. This fragrant wake accompanies me, mingling with the lingering taste of chocolate on my tongue, in the pieces of German words I am slowly forgetting. All this instils in me a joyous yet melancholy high.

Swallowing hard, I slow my descent then stop to stand on the next landing; rooted, my hand insists on gripping the banister as I look around. The scent endures, feels all-encompassing like the peal of the twin-steeple church when I am strolling near the river. I have entered into it as it continues to billow all around me.

There are no other footsteps on the floorboards, no other doors closing or even signifying someone has been by.

And then ... my mind conjures up only *her.*

The perfume slowly begins to fade yet I want to wait it out longer. But what if someone opens their door and finds me here, standing stupidly, sniffing around like a crazed and lost vagrant? What would my unknown neighbours say, what kind of shocked expression would pass over their eyes—and would I even under-stand them if they only spoke *Sorbisch,* the dialect of the outlying region? Decisively I continue my descent and oh, another painful wafting of that fragrance! I begin to dread the ground floor, my own apartment.

***

To this day, I don't know how Tosia could have smelled so lovely at the age of six; perhaps she routinely sneaked a few drops from her mother's perfume bottle or maybe it *wasn't* perfume? How would I know? I was only six. Somehow the feeling of being six has never quite left me, especially when it is snowing and the afternoon clouds are tinged soft orange and pale white. The trees are bare and the school bell has rung, calling us all in.

There are the desks, the rows that seemed long and the black-board, which was dark green.

Tosia.

I smile. At the beginning of the school year, while reading out the attendance list, our grade one teacher mispronounced her name. "*Toe-zia?*"

"*Tosha,*" the small voice asserted across the room. Then, in win-ter, she sat beside me.

We stood still for the National Anthem and for the Lord's Prayer; she was the only one who would recite the latter in Polish. Stealing a glance, raising my head, I can see her now, head lowered, eyes closed, small but full lips mouthing those sacred—*to her*—words.

When the prayer was over, she opened her eyes, glanced over to me.

We didn't go to the same church; in fact, I didn't go to church at all. In grade three, my parents moved away from Ghent St. and I was sent to the public school. Besides, they didn't see the purpose of sending me to Catholic school—my father especially, as my parents were conflicted by their own religious upbringings (my dad a lapsed Dutch Reform, my mother, the faintest of Ukrainian Catholics).

But *Ojcze Nasz*—'Our Father'—I hear those words now with this scent as I bow my head, my footsteps once again coming to a standstill.

Tosia in a white winter jacket, the hood fringed with faux-white fur; cheeks red, nose running and sniffling, the chilled afternoon air on her skin. We played on the ice and then the bell rang; I would take my boots off beside her in the back room, hang my coat up next to hers, our sleeves snug against each other.

In grade three we moved and then, years later, when I was friends with my neighbour, Christina, Tosia was in her class and they would do math homework together. That confident scent assailed me again like a bouquet of flowers so lovely, so welcoming. I escaped the after-dinner arguments between my parents and, when I walked into Christina's house, the screen door shushing behind me, Tosia's scent would rush up to meet me. Sometimes, while I was climbing the cement steps of the stoop, my nose could already pick up a faint trace of it waiting for me on the threshold.

Inside, seemingly in another world, I saw her sitting at the large kitchen table. Sometimes she'd look up, pencil in hand, hair shorter, just down to her neck but still those green eyes and high cheeks. It was a look that made me feel like we were six again, as if she had caught me looking at her during prayer. Or when I snuck glances at her math work, her threes and twos rounder than mine. I can still see the nape of her neck under the bright amber cast of the dining room lamp.

Tosia. There she'd be, books spread out, Christina on the phone in her bedroom, a giant, silver pot still simmering on the stove, red-orange rings of marinara on their plates, crumbs on the tablecloth. Mrs. Patini always let her daughter's friends stay for dinner if they wanted. Did I want some? I often did as I felt too tense to eat at my own dinner table.

Then, when autumn came, the maples on our street turned a bright red and orange, the sky crisp with that sunny but sweet cooler air. And behind the façades of bungalows and side-split houses we heard the loud, boisterous conversations of our Italian neighbours as they picked grapes from their rows of suburban, backyard vines. Looking at Tosia, I prayed to have such afternoons in our future.

At Christina's I didn't have to worry about Tosia overhearing my parents when their voices rose. With Tosia on my friend's stoop, the homework and the dinners done, the autumn days darkening early and the smell of burning leaves lifting in the air, a hint of smoke from someone's backyard mingled with Tosia's scent so perfectly changeless; it wafted over to me like a hand that leads you through a crowd. For a while, a bit of Tosia lingered on my sleeve even though she had long arisen from the stoop, long given me her hug goodbye. After those brief embraces, I often sat on the stoop, staring down at the grass, realizing I could never hold on long enough. Forever relishing those hugs, those moments of Tosia looking over her shoulder, past her blonde hair at the wan yellow light falling through Christina's screen door.

Away from her, the scent was a form of consolation. When it was gone, I always knew it was time to go home.

***

I didn't go to the same high school as Tosia and Christina. But one winter night when I was fifteen, Tosia showed up at my door. She stood in the alcove, happily breathing out small clouds of cold air, surrounded by the girls I once knew, girls I once danced with at the old Y and yes, Tosia, too, had been there.

She wore white earmuffs, a pony-tail and something different, another scent, something lighter, like almonds. We went for a winter-night walk, Tania and Anna behind us joking about Jessica's new boyfriend; I stuttered, trying to find something to say, reeling from the shock of Tosia's presence. Suddenly I remembered her white coat from grade one. Did she? Of course, and she asked me if I still picked my nose under my desk. I laughed, that was a game I played, pretending to drop my pencil only to sneak one good pick, my eager finger in either nostril, out for a new find but she saw me once and wagged a tawny finger to reprimand me.

She lifted that same finger—though it was longer, more slender —at me again on our walk, and then, at Linlake Park, we stopped where half the soccer field stood frozen, surrounded by clumps of grass like the ragged scalps of half-buried men. On the ice we were six years old again, sliding across.

When she asked about my parents, I pretended not to hear.

I saw her again the following summer at Marzena's sixteenth birthday party; I didn't know they were cousins until that afternoon. Tosia had invited me on the phone though I really didn't know Marzena that well. I later understood she and her family had just that year arrived to Canada, that her father had worked in Gdańsk. Tosia's father and her father were brothers, that was all I could catch that afternoon.

Later, Marzena's neighbours, a fat, older couple, invited us all over for a swim in their kidney-shaped pool. Tosia in her silver-blue one-piece walked across Marzena's front lawn, the cicadas a wall of sound reverberating in the wild humid day. She looked taller than I ever seemed to remember, her legs the colour of rain-dampened sand and she had breasts and slender arms yet why did it seem so surprising? Somehow, by walking across the yellowed-grass in her bare feet, she was performing some minute miracle that I alone witnessed.

I cannot remember another time when I felt such a jittering in my knees, such weakness in my shins; a pleasurable nausea rose up in my chest. It was a discovery, a waking up that terrified yet electrified me.

When I was close to her in the pool, Paulo performing a cannonball, she turned her head away from the splash erupting like a volcano. Her green eyes squinted then widened a little and she smiled at me. I felt the water on my face, and amidst the scent of chlorine and vanilla suntan lotion on her tanned shoulders, I felt safe.

***

I will say, there was an 'almost' moment between us. There had to have been.

I was sitting in the backseat of my parents' car, alone on a Friday. In the already darkened October evening, the red and orange leaves appeared dark and pale. My father had just parked the car in the quieter back lot of a plaza near the Catholic high school. He got out to go to the liquor store while my mother went to the pharmacy to pick up a prescription. We had just come from our favourite Italian restaurant and it was strange; a week after they announced the separation, we followed through on the Friday routine of dinner out and of my father picking up beer on the way home.

And in my waiting, I heard voices, laughing and running. I couldn't make out the faces at first but one voice sounded like Paulo, another like Lori, Jessica and yes, Christina. They were in the shadow of a maple tree that stood in front of a lamp.

Suddenly, there was Tosia walking out of the shadow, turning around, pausing. She stopped and leaned against the plaza wall, looking one way then the other, hands behind her back.

She wasn't far and I wondered if she sensed me there in the backseat. I wanted so desperately to get out and go to her but I didn't. I thought of my parents and what they had done to each other and felt so afraid for myself. It seemed impossible that the little girl in grade one, the one who bowed her head in prayer, could close her eyes in a kiss—for someone like me. I didn't feel I deserved her.

And even now I can feel that backseat surrounding me, and how I knew then that that moment would be all I would have of Tosia. It was maybe five minutes, the crickets chirping, autumn on its way and a passing shudder of a car on the road. Then suddenly Tosia looked over towards the car. I could feel her eyes. Quickly, I dropped my head, hoping not to be seen, embarrassed that I had been with my parents, hoping she would run off or be dragged away when her friends returned.

***

The next time I saw her, I was waiting in line at the cinema and she was with another boy. She stood further up ahead, the boy pulling out his wallet to pay for them at the box office. Since I was watching a film with my mother, I prayed we wouldn't sit in the same theatre as them. My cheeks felt like the heavy slabs of the cement sidewalk I waited upon.

For the longest time, like a child that only sees things in terms of themselves, I stupidly continued to believe she existed purely for me. Instead of seeing her for her, I regarded Tosia as an extension of myself, as the ideal that would remain and wait—only for me. Yet, at the movies I realized Tosia was growing up, she had to and maybe I hadn't. She had crossed a kind of threshold while I lingered, afraid of adulthood.

And after that, I don't know what happened to her. I moved away from St. Catharines, making a point of losing touch. I had a falling out with my father. It is ridiculous the things I blamed him for. I realized as I got older the separation wasn't easy for him.

Years later, I was in Toronto, sitting on the subway. It was winter, a white scarf wrapped around my neck, when I saw a young woman up ahead with the same cheeks as Tosia, the same tawny skin. She tenderly cradled a baby in a snug winter coat, a carriage near the door. This mother cooed to her crying child in a Slavic tongue; I thought it was Polish. I tried to listen to her, watch her as the train rocked us along, but the Muslim woman behind me barked at her daughter. At the next station the young mother got off, carriage wheels clattering over the steel threshold, the door closing on her; on the other side of the glass she continued to calm her child, remnants of Slavic words barely reaching my ears.

***

I took a course enabling me to teach English in Europe—in Wrocław. I rented a small apartment, all I could afford, and all the Polish girls in the *rynek,* the town square, resembled Tosia. But I didn't get close to any. An American friend, wanting to get me laid, took me one night to a café where waitresses, dressed in traditional garb, chained patrons to their chairs. Karl ate a raspberry from a large girl's tanned cleavage. She looked away from him, her eyes brown, lids blinking bored but sad. She quickly backed away the moment his mouth touched down on her skin. I averted my eyes, feeling sorry for the tourists at the other tables, who chuckled and hollered lewd encouragement in other languages.

***

I had so many fantasies; they followed me in my daydreams.

Then, after three months, the school cancelled my contract, then filed for bankruptcy without any warning so I was forced to leave.

On my last afternoon in Poland, I ate a lonely farewell lunch at my favourite restaurant, Kurna Chata, had three fast pints of *Piast.* Outside, it rained then snowed. I walked back to the centre and around the square under the grey-blue sky, looking at the pastel buildings one last time, my cheeks wet while the tourists bought their trinkets and ornaments in the Christmas market. The flakes turned back into drops and then stopped falling. Even the puddles seemed perfect and in the distance a bell coldly gonged, the sound matching the silvered ripples the wind made in those tiny lakes.

Then, in Plac Solny, the verdant aroma of stems and petals knitted together to form a kind of blanket around me. Circling the flower vendors, hearing their muddled conversations, maybe a little high from the beer, I felt myself looking for her, as if we were supposed to meet so she could give me her hand.

"*Ojcze Nasz*," and those eyes that once looked over to me.

So, seemingly rootless, I came to Germany. Jolanta, one of my students in Poland, had a sister living in Görlitz, a city which I was told would suit me.

And it does, it is a beautiful but quiet city. I teach the young and old, mostly those in the tourist industry. But early evenings I walk to the border, the arbitrary border and I cross the river, the Lusatian Neisse. *Nysa Łużycka* and I'm in Poland and I tell myself, it's different. *It is.* There, I take in the unfolding dusk smelling of wet cobbles and passing cars. Still, I look at the old buildings, the ancient bricks and the bare trees, my hands deep in my pockets, the world feeling both colder and kinder.

I meander along the river then go to the café on ulica Partyzantów where I slowly sip German wine, watching the park across the street darken then disappear. I always try to carry twenty *złoty* in my wallet.

This is all I need.

***

And now, as I stand here, the perfume is almost gone. My foot lifts off the wooden stair, one last crack, one last insurmountable sense of wonder and loss and then, the ground floor. Up above, I hear a lock, the click, then the crack of hinges, strange voices and now I can smell fried onions, an aroma I would love if it didn't mean I must completely lose this one.

Maybe tonight, I'll go to Poland again. Key in hand, I nod to no one but myself.

I need my winter coat.

HAPPILY EVER AFTER

Corinne Wasilewski

I'M ONE PART Irish, one part French, one part German, and one part Polish. The Irish in me keeps a low profile. It goes back five generations and manifests itself in predictable ways—my tolerance for cold and damp, for example. When the fog moves in off the Bay of Fundy, beads on my hair and skin, runs down my forehead and drips off my nose, I don't even think to put up my hood. That's the bulk of my Irish legacy, as far as I know. That and my affinity for fisherman knit sweaters.

My obsession with order comes from the German. I fold my underwear in half, then in quarters, and stack them in my drawer by colour, completely separate from my socks.

And from the French, what? My weakness for french fries with gravy? It's a bit of a stretch, I know. Not that it matters. I'm Polish through and through. Even now with Babcia gone, it's Poland I see when I close my eyes. Poland with its mermaids, dragons and Prince Charming look-a-likes. And don't forget castles. A real life never-never land.

"What do you want to be when you grow up?" adults would ask when I was small. "Polish," I'd say. They'd chuckle, a restrained chuckle—half amusement-half bewilderment. "But, you're Canadian."

"Polish is better." I'd hold the hands of a pretend prince, and pirouette in his arms. to *The Wonderful World of Disney* theme song turned up in my head.

Then again, anywhere was probably better than Pennfield, where there's no royal ball, no prince, no palace, and the men have short stubby fingers and the build and grace of refrigerators. Where the closest thing to a castle is the Algonquin Hotel in St. Andrews.

Fifty years and Babcia never felt at home here. She'd be on the beach digging clams or in the field raking blueberries, one hand on a rake, and one hand swatting flies, when she'd suddenly go quiet, and stand perfectly still. "I miss Poland," she'd whisper, eyes fixed on the horizon and a berry-stained hand pressed to her heart.

I'd put down my rake and wrap my arms around her legs. Poor Babcia. At least I was used to vast, empty spaces; endless sea, endless sky, endless trees; used to life at the end of the world; used to feeling alone. Not Babcia. She grew up in a very old house in a very old square in the centre of a town called Płock. The house was finished in pink stucco with troubadours painted on the gable and the square teemed with people all hours of the day and night.

She really didn't belong in New Brunswick. For one thing, she was the only woman I knew who put on lipstick to do chores. And she had long hair down to her waist in the purple colour of Dark Harbour dulse. She braided it in a coil on top of her head so that it looked like a crown. She wore silk stockings—even in summer—that clipped to a garter. She was in another league. Nobody in Pennfield gave her the respect she deserved. People here thought she was weird.

Every night before I went to sleep, I prayed for Babcia. I prayed that God in his infinite wisdom would find a way to get her back to Poland. I prayed to go there, too. I also wished on new pennies, chicken bones, four-leafed clovers, and shooting stars. To cover all the bases, I opened up a bank account and started saving money. By the time I reached high school I was earning double-digit interest and stocking up on travel books—the free ones you could get at Marlin Travel.

That's when Babcia developed heart problems. Her entire body began to shut down. In the end she had to sleep sitting up and the pulse in her neck fluttered non-stop like a hummingbird was stuck inside. Her feet swelled to watermelons and her breaths were all squish and suck like rubber boots in a mud puddle. I pictured her a sinking ship, water rising to her ankles, then knees, then chest, slowly filling her entire body. All we could do was watch her go down.

We cremated Babcia and put her on the mantelpiece between my mother's Pied Piper and Orange Seller Royal Doulton figurines. Cremation was Babcia's idea; the mantelpiece, my mother's.

The dreams started six months later. At first I blamed them on pizza too close to bedtime. Or on sour cream and onion chips with dill pickle dip. Or on the cat asleep on my feet. But when the dreams didn't stop, I knew it meant something more.

The dreams were all the same: Babcia straight and tall, shoulders square, forty-two D breasts thrust forward and arms stretched out in an odd combination of the Queen Mother and the risen Christ at his Ascension. There were no props, no clues as to location. She hovered in mid-air or maybe outer space. It was hard to tell. There were no stars, no moon, no satellites. Only a breeze that pulled tendrils of hair from her elegant braid and lifted the skirt of her A-line dress with the polka-dot print to reveal saggy knees and the dull metal of her garters. "Anna," she called. "Anna." It was a new tone for Babcia. A "get-off-your-lazy-ass-and-do-something" tone, more like my mother's. Even so, she must have come to me twelve or thirteen times before I finally got the message.

Against my parents' wishes, I emptied my bank account and booked a flight to Poland. The night before I left, I filled an empty pickle jar with Babcia's ashes. Not just any pickle jar, but the one for *Polskie ogórki* in brine. I put the jar in a plastic bag, rolled it in our thickest towel, and packed it in the middle of my suitcase. On top I laid my prom dress, my black patent leather shoes with the velvet bows which I'd worn only once, and my crystal chandelier earrings.

***

Płock was different than I'd imagined. For one thing it was grey, the colour of a smudge that's left on paper when you rub out a mistake.

I stayed in a hotel on the edge of the Old Town. The view from the balcony was concrete with a splash of red from a window box across the courtyard. My room was lime green with yellow baseboards and trim. I set my suitcase on the bed and began to unpack. First, my prom dress. I lifted it high and shook out the wrinkles. It was tight through the bodice and then full at the hips with a hem that skimmed the floor. I held it close and circled the room in fast, head-spinning turns that streaked the light in the overhead fixture. I waltzed through the open door and out onto the balcony, where I plopped on a stool all out of breath.

Soon the sun dipped behind a red roof. Swallows appeared by the hundreds, soaring and diving like planes at an airshow. I watched, loving it, but not amazed. This was Poland, after all. Poland, not Canada. Płock, not Pennfield. When my eyes spied a turret through the branches of a giant willow, I almost cried. This felt like home to me. This was where I belonged. I leaned against the wall, wrapped my arms around my legs, and waited for the magic to start.

***

My alarm clock went off at nine o'clock the next morning. I heard its muffled beeps and struggled to awareness. So this was jet lag: a head packed in bubble wrap, my eyes duct taped shut, and ten pound weights strapped to each limb. If not for my meeting with Marek Kowalski, I'd have ignored the noise and slept the day away. Instead, I dragged my feet to the bathroom with my fingers propping up my eyelids.

I was nervous about meeting Marek. He was Babcia's best friend's grandson and his *Babcia* had laid down the law, or so I imagined, and insisted he be my host for the week. Or maybe he'd taken a whole week off work in support of my cause of his own free will (enter knight in shining armour stage right). Either way I was lucky—he being a rare breed, a Pole who spoke English.

We had made plans to meet at The Ombre at ten. I walked in

and did a slow pan of the room. The décor was simple, sombreros on the walls with pictures of iguanas filling the gaps and a photograph of Pope John Paul II over the bar. A waiter stepped forward and addressed me in Polish. "Something-or-other Marek Kowalski," he said. I nodded and followed him into a cavern-like recess at the back of the room where the pale face of a man materialized in the gloom, his bald head hovering inches above the table top, his miniature feet dangling above the floor. I rubbed my eyes and looked again.

"Anna Watson?" he asked.

"Yes."

He hopped down from his chair. "Marek Kowalski at your service."

The top of his head came to my belly button and I wasn't even in my high heels. "Pleased to meet you." I set my purse on the table and put out my hand.

"The pleasure is all mine." He lifted my hand to his lips with a graceful sweep of his arm. "It is a very great honour to make the acquaintance of a woman from America."

"I'm not American. I'm Canadian, which reminds me." I pulled my hand free of his fingers which had continued to clasp mine despite the fact we were past introductions, and went digging in my shoulder bag. "This is for you." I set a tin log cabin of maple syrup in the middle of the table.

"Please do not suppose I harboured expectations of a present." He picked up the tin and squinted at the label. "Canada #1 Medium Pure Maple Syrup. Of course, I am a diabetic, but this is not so important. It is the thought that is central. Let me inform you that I esteem this gift very much. Now please to sit down."

I picked up a menu. Marek waved it away. "May I propose the beef burritos?" he said.

"I was thinking of something Polish."

"I am having a Żywiec. Perhaps it would satisfy your notion?"

"Excuse me?"

"It's Polish beer—very cultural."

"I'll just have coffee and a doughnut, thanks."

Marek leaned back in his chair and clasped his hands behind his head as though The Ombre was an office and the table was his desk. Between his abbreviated body and bald head I couldn't tell if he was ten or one hundred and ten.

"You have come a long way to bring your *Babcia* home," he said. "You have come a long way, and not only this, you have committed many sacrifices. Number one, you have sacrificed currency. Number two, time. Also, you have sacrificed your tongue, your friends and relations, and your well acquainted way of life. Last of all—and this is the grand condensation—you have sacrificed all your security. It is a very great number to sacrifice and proof you are a peculiar woman, a brave woman, a woman with a good heart. And I, I am your devoted servant." At this point he must have propped his feet against the pedestal leg of the table because the table, and everything on it, suddenly lurched forward into my ribcage, except for my purse, which fell over on its side and sent Babcia's ashes rolling across the tabletop and right off the edge.

"Babcia!" I couldn't even make a grab for her; the table held me prisoner. If not for the quick reflexes of the waiter who managed to juggle the tray with our order in one hand while catching the pickle jar with the other, Babcia's remains might have found a permanent resting place at The Ombre. He was a real athlete, our waiter—a long-distance runner with his long legs and lean body. But I think it was his fingers that saved the day. His incredible E.T.-like fingers just slipped under that jar and scooped it up like he was fielding a grounder.

"Thank you, thank you." I clutched Babcia to my chest and then gently set her on the table beside the salsa.

Marek looked at the jar, then at me, and then back at the jar. "That's a prodigious pickle jar," he said. He lit up a cigarette, clamped it tight between his lips and then pulled a picture from the breast pocket of his shirt. "Your *Babcia* was a beautiful woman." He slid the photograph across the table to me. "Do you know you have her eyes?"

I picked up the photo and held it to the light of the TV. The girl in the picture couldn't have been more than twenty. She wore a high necked blouse with lace at the throat and shoulders that accentuated the curve of her braid. It was true that she was beautiful, although she had a rounder face than the woman I remembered. Also a wider smile. She looked almost happy. I handed the photo back to Marek. "It's wonderful."

He shook his head. "It's for you to keep, a portrait of your Babcia as a young woman."

I slipped the picture back into my purse. "Thank you." I took a sip of coffee, the worst I'd ever tasted. The grounds settled between my teeth and in the grooves at the base of my gums. I pushed the cup away and concentrated on the doughnut.

"Those things will slay you," Marek said, pointing to my doughnut. "Better you don't eat it."

He laid some złotys on the table. "Today I take you to the place your Babcia lived."

I abandoned my doughnut, returned Babcia to my purse and followed him out.

"Will you burden me with your pocketbook?" he asked.

"It's not heavy," I said, lying.

We cut through a narrow alley that connected to a square, although to be honest, the square was really more a rectangle. Run-down patrician houses bordered the cobblestone, some turned into restaurants and cafés, and in front of these stood giant chestnut trees, and in the centre, a water fountain and a stage swarming with skateboarders. We walked up the long side of the rectangle, my eyes on the lookout for a certain pink house with troubadours on the front, my feet pushing through leaves that looked like rheumatoid hands.

"The trees have a plague and will soon be eradicated," Marek said.

We walked on in silence for fifty metres or so.

"There." He pointed to a patchwork house of brick and stucco; a vacant house with broken glass, peeling paint, and rotting woodwork.

I pulled Babcia's ashes out of my shoulder bag and carried them close enough to touch the crumbling mortar. Apparently someone had plastered over the troubadours somewhere along the line and there wasn't a trace of pink to be seen. "What about here?" I whispered to Babcia. "Is this the place?" I waited for Babcia to give me a sign. I was open to anything—thermodynamics, mental telepathy, acts of God.

"Presently, they will ravage this house along with two others and produce a hotel here instead," Marek called from the cobblestone.

I stood up on tiptoe and peered through a window. Chip bags, orange rind, soiled diapers, and every imaginable form of human waste lay knee deep on the floor. I plugged my nose and turned away. "This isn't the place," I said.

***

The next day Marek picked me up at the hotel. "Before I forget, this is for you." I handed him a plastic ROOTS bag with the picture of the beaver on the outside.

"I hope so you realize I did not harbour expectations of a present." He pulled out the T-shirt and held it to his chest. It hung to his knees. "Red is my beloved colour."

"I'm sorry it's so big. I didn't know your size."

"Do not be distressed. I have found spacious clothes to be effective on occasion, chiefly after a vast meal." He folded the shirt carefully and returned it to the bag. "Shall we go?"

The cemetery was too far to walk so we took Marek's scooter. Inside the wall it was graves as far as the eye could see, graves set above the earth like great beds of stone.

The Drozdowski family plot was engulfed in weeds. We trampled the grass to reveal three names: Władysław 1890-1945, Maria 1893-1970, and Adam 1926-1944—Babcia's parents and her only brother. Babcia's ashes weighed heavy on my shoulder. I took them out of my purse and set them on the grave. "What do you think?" I whispered. "Is this the place?" I stared at the pickle jar and waited for a sign. Nothing. "Come on, Babcia. Make up your mind." No response. "This isn't the place," I said to Marek.

***

The day before I left, Marek and I walked to the New Town. It wasn't so new, six hundred years old to be exact. Just newer than the Old Town. It was my final stop. I'd seen everything else: the castle overlooking the Vistula, the cathedral with its Romanesque architecture, the section of old city wall where Babcia had her first kiss, and the forest where she searched for mushrooms—except the trees had been cleared to make room for apartment blocks after the war. I'd seen all these places and Babcia's answer was always the same. Silence. Pure silence.

***

That night I had a dream: Babcia standing in the blueberry field back home, one hand on a rake, one hand swatting flies. In the background, her house with the pale green siding, and beyond that a shimmering sliver of sea. She swatted a fly on her bare shin, then looked up and smiled a wide, toothy grin. Her hair was hanging loose and the wind made it ripple like water. She raised an arm and gestured me to come.

ROSETTA

David Huebert

EVERYWHERE PAUL LOOKED he saw tanned young girls in orange short shorts handing out Jägermeister bandanas and sunglasses. He'd waddled through the security gates with a mickey of whiskey in his groin and by the time the sun set he was more than buzzed.

During a break between bands, he wandered off to get some fish and chips. He was dousing his fries with malt vinegar when he spotted her, sitting by herself on a little hump of grass, hugging her knees and staring out over the harbour. She had a mess of black curls and her jean shorts showed long, pale legs.

When she saw him looking, she smiled. For a moment Paul wondered whether they had met before, but he knew they hadn't. She patted the grass beside her and he was surprised when he went over, sat down. She took one of the fries from his cardboard plate and, munching it, said: "What do you want to say to me?"

"Sorry?"

"What would you say, right now, if you could say anything you want?"

Paul watched a tugboat gliding through the twilit harbour. "I'd ask how old you are."

"That it?"

"Guess so. Maybe I'd offer you a fry."

She laughed, showing half-chewed potato on her tongue. When she saw Paul looking at her mouth, she raised a hand to cover it.

"What would you say, to me?"

She squinted, thinking. "I'd say you should shave the beard."

She put her fingers to his cheek, played soft keyboard across his chin. "You've got a strong jaw."

There was a deep crackle from the stage and a cheer from the crowd. The girl jumped to her feet as a violinist started to warm up. "It's Hey Rosetta," she said, setting out towards the stage. "They're so fun!"

Paul stood up. "What's your name?"

She looked over her shoulder, beaming. "Rosetta!" she shouted, and ran away giggling.

"Wait," he called, but she was already half way to the stage.

With some effort, Paul managed to keep himself from following her. He ate his fish and chips and then went to the beer tent to meet up with the friends he'd come over from Halifax with. They sipped Canadian from plastic cups and leaned on the fence as they watched Hey Rosetta. Darkness fell and some clouds moved in. Occasionally the crowd parted and he saw her black curls bouncing beneath the purple lights or her thin arms pitched high in the air. But he tried not to watch her. When Hey Rosetta finished their set, he finished his beer and headed off to find a toilet.

He was walking back towards the stage when he felt a few drops spatter his forearm. Soon after that the air was thick with rain. The Jägermeister girls ran around handing out makeshift raincoats and before long the crowd was a sea of neon orange ponchos. Broken Social Scene came out and started to warm up and Paul went to the front of the stage, where an overhang gave some shelter.

When the band started to play, everyone pushed up front, dancing in the summer rain, the steady beat and the eerie melody changing them from people into a crowd. Paul took his flask out and had a long pull and there she was, black curls bobbing right in front of him. He tapped her on the shoulder and she turned, flushed and beaming. She took the flask from his hands and drained it, handing it back with a grin.

She threw her arms in the air and he put his hands on her hips and they were dancing together, dancing fast as the drums thumped and rumbled.

On the ferry home he asked again how old she was.

"Old enough," she said.

At that moment, it was the sweetest thing he'd ever heard.

***

In August, a few days after the Alderney Landing concert, he got the call from Chebucto High. They had an opening for a long-term French sub, a maternity leave position. Every teacher in the city wanted to work at Chebucto, so he was astonished that they'd called him. He was still more shocked when the interview turned out to be more of a meet-and-greet.

Mrs. Turner, the head of the arts department, asked him a few questions about mutual acquaintances from the Mount. Then they talked about King's College, where Paul had done his undergrad. Mrs. Turner's son was a rugby player, going into his second year at King's.

She didn't ask any questions about his resumé. He wasn't asked to speak a word of French. He made no use of the hours he'd spent reviewing his classroom management strategies and philosophy of education. But none of this bothered Paul once Mrs. Turner brought him to the office and presented him with a nine month contract and, after he'd signed it, said: "See you in September."

***

"My son? Employed? Nothing short of a miracle."

Paul's father, Roman, was reclining in a Muskoka chair, looking out over his backyard and cradling a vodka on the rocks. The house was a tall Victorian in the South End. Although he developed and sold condos for a living, Roman had never lived in one. When clients asked him about this he answered vaguely, usually blaming his Polish blood. But Paul knew why his father needed to sleep on the ground floor. The older man woke up several nights a week, dreaming that his house was burning down.

"Hilarious, Dad. I worked all year last year."

"I didn't say *worked*. I said *employed*."

"Jesus," Paul's mother called from the kitchen. "Take it easy. We're celebrating."

"Yes, Jacinthe, of course, we are. We're celebrating the fact that our son is finally employed, after years of drifting and mooching and burdening his parents."

"You mean studying and earning degrees?" Paul asked.

Roman rose from his chair. "Precisely." He slurped the rest of his vodka before heading inside to pour more liquor over the same unmelted cubes.

They had tourtière for dinner. Whenever there was any excuse for celebration, his mother made tourtière, though no one in the family particularly liked it. Roman did not speak during the meal, although he did get up twice to refresh his drink. The second time, Paul gave his mother a look, but she kept her eyes on her plate. As Paul's sister Maria was clearing the dishes, his mother turned to him. "So: any girlfriends or boyfriends?" Since his ex, Maya, had gone off to med school at Western, his mother seemed afraid Paul would never date again.

Roman watched his son with a level gaze. No matter how much vodka the older man put back he never showed any sign of drunkenness.

"Well, there is someone. Met her at a concert last week."

"Lovely," Jacinthe said. "What's her name?"

Paul swallowed realizing that he could not answer. "Rosetta," he said.

"Rosetta." His mother smiled. "What a lovely name."

***

Paul's second class as a Chebucto teacher was grade ten core French. It was the last period before lunch and he was hungry and fatigued. He read over his notes as his students streamed in and took their seats. He'd made up his mind not to look up until they got settled, but then he caught sight of her black curls and his head lifted of its own accord.

The bell rang and Paul stood to introduce himself to the class. He felt her look and it took everything not to meet her eyes. In French, he thanked the students for being there and told them his name. Then he began the attendance, still sensing her eyes on him. The sheet shook in his hands and he felt sweat gathering in his lower back.

When he called out the name "Lisa Tremblay," she raised her arm.

"Hey," she said, completely casual. "You shaved your beard." A bunch of the students laughed.

Paul didn't say anything. He stumbled through the remaining names, managing not to look at her. After lamely outlining the first unit of the year he handed out a crossword and staggered around the room, offering vacuous help and avoiding her gaze. The world was a punctured lung, gasping.

She remained at her desk after all the other students had left. The word "wrong" entered his head. Lisa stood and approached his desk and for the first time he saw her age in her stride.

"It looks good," she said.

"What?"

"Your face. Sans beard. It's better."

"You shouldn't talk to me like that. You can't."

She reached out, ran her fingers along his jaw. "But I like it. I'm allowed to like it, right?"

He did not say anything. He could not have explained why he let her fingers stay where they were, then reached up and took her hand in his.

After a time Paul asked: "Why didn't you ever call?"

"Why do you think?" She dropped his hand and headed towards the door. For a moment he thought she would leave the room, and a dark howl roared in his gut. But when she reached the door she pulled it shut, careful not to make a sound.

***

Paul was fourteen when he learned about the fire. Roman told the story in great detail that one time and they never discussed it again. Ten years later Paul still had no idea whether his sister or his mother knew. He did not remember the exact words his father had used, but he knew the story as if he himself had been there.

Roman had been drinking at his friend Marek's barn on the outskirts of Nysa. They were teenagers and this was something they did regularly on the weekends. The barn was a mile from the farmhouse and Marek's parents couldn't hear them carrying on in there. There were five boys there that night and one of them, Alek, had brought an enormous jar of home-brewed alcohol. They drank and smoked tobacco and laughed, as always, late into the night. Roman was the first to turn in so he went up to the loft and slept while the other boys carried on below.

He awoke to the smell of smoke and the sound of screaming, the heat closing in. Below, he heard human screams and the desperate groan and squeal of livestock. Roman was alone in the loft. He could feel the fire but he couldn't see it. There was nothing but darkness and the swirl of smoke. He leaned over the edge of the loft and felt around with his palms, hoping to find somewhere he could jump off. But the heat was churning and rising all around him.

He put his back on the floor of the loft and placed his bare heels on the inside of the roof. The smoke was tiring him now and his breath was ragged. He pulled both legs back and kicked as hard as he could, trying to ignore the screams.

He kicked again and again as the barn grew hotter and the space seemed to shrink. His lungs seized up and he found that he could not regain his breath. He put everything into his heels, pounding them into the roof, thinking only about each thrust. Thump. Thump.

His feet crashed through the roof and the cold air rushed inside. He stuck his face out, gasping, his mouth wide open. He saw

Marek and another boy standing below. Marek was keeled over, coughing and wheezing. The other boy had his head raised to the sky and he saw Roman at the window. He waved his arms and shouted, telling him to jump.

Roman felt the heat on his back, drawing closer. He listened to the screams and the crackling of wood and hay. He closed his eyes and leapt.

He landed on his feet, cracking his head on his right knee.

Roman awoke to the sound of sirens. There was a lot of shouting, and then two men in blue uniforms were putting him in a stretcher and some other men were struggling to put the fire out. Roman faded in and out of consciousness. The sun was beginning to rise when he saw them carrying the bodies out of the smouldering barn. Two of them, the colour of cast iron.

***

Paul was in bed with Lisa when the phone rang. Before she spoke he could hear the sob in his mother's voice. Then: "It's your father."

Paul learned the full story gradually. Roman had tried to go to bed but he was staggering and slurring and Jacinthe made him take a cold shower first. This was not unusual. She helped him into the shower and then left, giving him some privacy. As she walked away she heard a thud and raced back to the bathroom. She found him lying on his back on the tiles, muttering, his legs draped over the side of the tub. She cried out when she saw him but he got up and assured her he was fine. He seemed remarkably sober.

Roman dried himself off and went to bed and quickly dozed off. Jacinthe watched over him and before long he began to cough violently. She roused him and asked if he was all right but he could only mutter incoherently. When she saw that he was hacking up blood, she called an ambulance. By the time the paramedics arrived, he had lost consciousness.

The doctors informed the family that Roman had suffered an

alcohol-induced stroke. Upon admission to the hospital, his blood alcohol content had been 0.45%, a potentially fatal number. In the days that followed, the family began to investigate and found stashes of vodka all over Roman's world. Neat rows of pint bottles in his desk at the office. A reeking water bottle in his gym bag. A forty in the furnace room. A stash of quarts in a basement trunk.

Within a few days, Roman was able to breathe without assistance. The alcohol left his blood. A CT scan revealed a dark patch near his left temple, but the doctors were unable to say whether there was brain damage. They could not make that judgement until he returned to consciousness, and that could be weeks, months, more.

***

In the weeks that followed, Paul made an effort to think about his father. He tried to conjure positive thoughts, tried to remember the good moments, the moments when his father was young and energetic, full of love for his mother and baby sister. These moments had existed, Paul was sure of it. But they would not come to him.

Instead, what surfaced again and again was a memory of a family trip to Wentworth. Jacinthe was an expert skier and she had taken the kids a few times before she finally convinced Roman to come along. She and Maria were on the bunny hill and Paul, who had caught on to the sport quickly, offered to take his father up the mountain. Roman claimed to be a competent skier and refused to warm up on one of the easy slopes. But it only took a few turns for Paul to realize that his father was uneasy. "You okay?" Paul asked.

"Yes, yes, I'm fine. Go ahead."

Paul pointed his skis down the mountain and took a few turns, coming out onto a steep pitch, the headwall. This part was not easy for him and he had to focus as he worked down it. Just before the slope flattened out, he heard his father's voice behind him: "Paweł! Paweł!"

Paul's parents had stopped using his Polish name as soon as he had entered school. Now it sounded strange to him, almost insulting. He stopped and turned to look up the headwall and saw his father lying in the snow, head pointed down the slope. His skis were tangled up and one pole was fifteen feet up the run. He saw then that his father was struggling to get up, summoning all his strength. But he couldn't stand on his own.

Paul took his skis off and dug his toes into the snow, marching up the mountain to help his father.

***

A week or two before Christmas, Paul got an email from a member of the disciplinary committee of the Nova Scotia Department of Education. It was the email he had been dreading for months.

That afternoon Mrs. Turner called him into her office. She handed him a piece of paper. "Paul," she said, "there's been a complaint."

"A complaint?"

"This is out of my hands now. But I want to hear it from you."

"Want to hear what?"

She glared at him. "You know, Paul, if you're found to be sleeping with a student, you will never teach in this province again."

"Yes. I know."

"Well, are you sleeping with a student?"

Paul stared down at the complaint in his hand, the sheet of recycled paper that marked the end of this career. The room grew hot and his breath went short and he felt himself there, in the loft, the flames and smoke rising as the hay burned below. Exhaustion took hold of him as he fought for oxygen, his lungs shrinking with each breath. He heard the screams all around him, the shrieks of pigs and the brays of sheep and the howls of young men. The smoke rose up, rank with the smell of burning flesh.

Paul kicked and kicked, the desperation giving him enormous power. Finally the roof opened, a ragged window to the black night sky. He felt the rush of cold air, saw the ground twenty feet below.

He jumped, and something strange happened. The ground did not rush up to meet him. Instead, he floated upwards, farther and farther from the earth. He was soaring up through the cool night air, bathing in it, his eyes wide open. Paul looked up and saw a perfect half-moon and a glittering splash of stars. Looking down again, he saw that the burning barn was far, far below.

"Yes," he said to Mrs. Turner. "I am."

SCENES FROM AN IMAGINARY LIFE

Dawid Kołoszyc

Returns without Returns

From a certain point on, there is no more turning back.
That is the point that must be reached.
—FRANZ KAFKA, THE ZÜRAU APHORISMS

IS THIS, FINALLY, the meaning of exile? Neither solitude nor nostalgia, just a prolonged sense of perplexity, along with an imperfect split between a life lived and a life imagined—elsewhere.

And year after year spent among ghosts. Year after year of retracing my steps somewhere between several languages, several incarnations; of slipping into cracks between worlds, of dreaming in foreign tongues, making love in foreign tongues, getting lost in foreign tongues; of living with secrets that remain secrets only because they can't be spoken in foreign tongues. Year after year of impossible returns, of uncertain pilgrimages to places that have almost ceased to exist, only to find myself standing, again, in the midst of a familiar yet somehow ineffable landscape, pressing my face against a mirage. Or against the palm of someone's hand.

Years of ridiculous dreams filled with untouchable objects and words frozen on partly open lips. Of searching, among them, for names of misplaced friends; for the people we were and the people we tried to be. For awkward first incursions into the realm of the senses and the realm of the spirit. And for memories of a dead People's Republic—the one that gave me a life and deprived me of a life, forcing me to endlessly construct imaginary versions of it. For memories of hours passed in long queues outside empty supermarkets. Of songs and parades and portraits of dead heroes used to calm the trepidations in the hearts of the working masses; of tanks and police clubs used to reassure them of the necessity of their commitment to a common cause. For the titles of the three books I had borrowed from a public library to bring on a trip I did not know could only ever be a one-way affair; books I later sent back, not on account of any allegiance to socialist principles, but due to a rather naïve conviction that a crime committed against a library constitutes a significant step on the path to barbarism.

And to think now: all this just to arrive at the more or less banal realization that we are all constantly returning to some impossible place—a childhood experience, a town left behind, a lost love, a lost illusion, or, who knows, maybe even some broken off fragment of ourselves, what we used to be before we became what we no longer recognize as familiar. That, only insofar as we become exiles, does time acquire any significance for us; does language begin to feel like an inexplicable promise.

And so I continue the dubious task of filling pages with words that know nothing about me.

Self-Portrait with a Fish

All fish are mute ... one used to think. But who knows?
Isn't there at last a place where, without them, we would be able
to speak in the language of fish?
—RAINER MARIA RILKE, SONNETS TO ORPHEUS

It is written in one of the gospels that, immediately after his resurrection, Jesus asked for food and was offered broiled fish. The gospel doesn't tell what kind of fish it was and how Jesus felt about his first meal back among the living, only that he ate in silence. As is commonly known, stories about Jesus' life can be highly instructive, even for those who believe he was merely a man in search of the first word, and not a god in search of the last.

When I was a child, my mother used to say: "Children and fish were not meant to have a voice." She would say this, for instance, when I questioned my parents' decisions or annoyed them with observations that contradicted their firmest beliefs. Whenever, that is, I tried to have the last word. Ever since then, I have remained committed to learning the language of fish, whose mute character stands in such a peculiar contrast to the infinitely convoluted wanderings of human words.

Now imagine this scene. December '81. A small town in a small country ravaged by age and the nervous convulsions of history. A train arrives at an old train station in the middle of the night. A woman in search of her husband leads two children across a frozen landscape to her father's house—one of the large houses of blackened red brick facing the tracks, built a long time ago for railway workers and their families; houses with tall stoves covered by white or yellow tiles and basins and buckets in place of washrooms. And now a small family gathering. A burning Christmas tree, the result of my father's reckless experiment with fire. My mother's hands holding a flower vase filled with water. The People's Republic had just declared war on the people. Carp and vodka on the table.

And now imagine this dream: a formal dinner party, in the course of which I am served a live fish. Perplexed, I watch the fish flop around on my plate. To my further astonishment, none of the other guests seated at the long table appear to be aware of my predicament as they bite into their own perfectly grilled servings. In a desperate attempt to buy time, I initiate a conversation with two elderly women sitting next to me, only to realize that I have been moving my lips without uttering a sound. Having apparently grown impatient with my mute discourse, one of the women suddenly stabs the fish on my plate with her fork and says, calmly yet insistently: "*Mangez, monsieur.*"

No, I still haven't learned to speak in the language of fish. But the possibility continues to haunt me through the memory of that disconcerting dream, which even today makes my lips grow slightly numb.

And no, I am not amusing myself at your cost, dear reader; I am simply trying to mark the limits of my words. Mark them as precisely as possible in order that I may learn to remain mute without ceasing to speak. The gods, too, remain mute even under the most strenuous of circumstances and, for that reason, precise in their absence.

A World like Any Other

God has given you one face and you give yourselves another.
—WILLIAM SHAKESPEARE, *HAMLET*

Horacio Oliveira was wrong.

If words are like us, it's not because they were born with a single face, but because they wear many faces. They wear them awkwardly, as though unable to decide which one fits better. And their faces slip off anyway, just like our faces slip off. They slip off despite our best efforts to keep them attached, and we wonder endlessly in search of mirrors to fix them. We tear off fragments and add new fragments and stitch them together hoping they will hold, hoping they will stay as we want them to stay, regardless of the circumstance. Hoping they will not slip off when we sleep next to someone we love. Then they become wrinkled anyway, as though in obedience to some natural law that declares calmly: this is what happens with a face when you wage an endless war against it; when you bend it and cut it and stretch it in every direction imaginable.

This is what happens with words.

Speak to me, Horatio. Speak to me in your intangible language. Tell me about your face. Is it like any other? Does it flee from you without permission like all faces do and go wondering alone in search of sharp objects? Does it conceal a secret tomb guarded by two headless statues? Tell me about invisible relations and inexplicable gestures. About unheard thoughts and untouchable bodies. Tell me this is how we live, always beyond reach. Crumbs of memories and a few incomplete encounters with people whose presence always turns out to be at once perfectly accidental and perfectly necessary.

Tell me, and I will tell you again that our life is the flight of a moth across a strangely furnished room. A moth which, sooner or later, comes to rest on a windowpane, looking at a world it can't enter.

PUSHPINS

Douglas Schmidt

THE SOUTH CLASSROOM wall in Patryk's grade five class is covered with maps. On the world map, countries are as bright as Life Savers. Canada, the United States, Mexico, and South America are in the centre. Dotted lines join places across oceans like the trails of Spiderman's web. San Francisco and Tahiti. New York and Reykjavik. On the left and right hand sides of the map are the two halves of the Union of Soviet Socialist Republics sliced down the middle. Patryk's parents said that, when they were growing up in Poland, the USSR was in the *middle* of the map, and slices of Canada and the US were on either side.

Beside the world map, the map of Canada is made of older paper and has faded pastel provinces. From too many stabs from pointing sticks, southern Ontario looks like it's been chewed away, as if the Great Lakes are filled with acid.

Ms. Cowan changes the cardboard number on the Royal Bank calendar from October 19th to 20th. It's ten days to Halloween which falls on a Saturday this year, 1987. Patryk and his sisters might be able to stay out later than usual.

"I want you to start thinking about your costumes," Ms. Cowan says, then stops. "Unless you don't celebrate Halloween." Samantha is a Jehovah's Witness and doesn't even celebrate her birthday. There's always someone who doesn't fit in. Patryk knows what that feels like. When he started grade one, he barely spoke any English.

Patryk's parents slowly got used to Halloween, which is not celebrated in Poland. His mom still thinks it's a ghoulish day and she wonders why children need to go from house to house begging for candy. She says Halloween must have been created by candy makers and dentists.

***

At dinner, Patryk tells his parents and his sisters Paulina and Danika about his class putting green pushpins on the world map where each student in the class was born. Yellow pins are for the birthplaces of the students' brothers and sisters. White pins are for their parents, and black pins are for their grandparents. There are also purple pins on places students in the class have visited. Most pins are on Canada and some are on Europe, the Middle East, Asia, and the Caribbean. There are some on South America where Ms. Cowan travelled when she was young. Australia, Antarctica, and Greenland have no pins. And no one was born at sea.

Patryk is the only student who has most of his pins clustered in Europe, in Warsaw, Poland. There's another pin for his little sister Paulina, who was born in Scarborough.

"This is good idea," his mother says. She smiles and nods at Patryk, and looks at their father. "To learn about world." At the end of the day she's tired and forgets to say the *the's* and the *a's*.

"No, it is not," his father says. "You are Canadian now, Patryk, like all the children in your class."

"It's a project. We *have* to," Patryk says picking at the chicken on his plate.

His father has opinions about everything. Sometimes coming home means another social studies lesson. Patryk has heard his father say that countries on maps are inventions. They're like bodies that could get fatter or thinner or just disappear. Poland is on the map, but his father says it isn't a real country right now, not the way Polish people want it to be. It hasn't been for a long time, his father says, it's just a puppet of the USSR.

Patryk imagines that everyone in Poland has puppet strings

attached to their arms and legs that come from the USSR. Patryk has also heard there's an iron curtain. He pictures the metal curtain creaking open so people outside can see the puppet show.

"One thing we want to know about Mizz Cowan," his mom says, giggling. "What is a *Mizz?*"

His father starts to laugh. "And if she's so Mizzerable," he asks, "what would make her happy?" His parents start laughing together, and talking quickly in Polish. Patryk knows they're making fun of Canadian things and people. They keep laughing until they're crying. Paulina laughs too but then goes to play with her dolls. Even she can tell that their parents are being silly.

At least their parents are laughing and not fighting. Patryk squirms. His parents say they don't understand why so many Canadians smile all the time and say: "Have a nice day." His mom says this makes Canadians seem stupid and simple.

Danika looks at him. She smiles just a little bit then looks at their parents, rolls her eyes, and smirks.

Smirk is a word she taught him. *Smirk* is an English word that sounds Polish. A smirk is a frown pushing down against a smile pushing up. And they're almost evenly matched. But the smile wins by just a little.

***

On the edges of the Ontario classroom map there are pictures showing different kinds of economic production like the farming of vegetables and tobacco, fishing, and manufacturing. Arrows from these pictures point to Ontario's cities and regions. Ms. Cowan told them that to her, Ontario looks a set of bagpipes. Ontario is the bag and the arrows are the pipes.

Patryk doesn't want to look at the map of Ontario because it makes him think of a heart with arrows stuck in it, like the sacred heart of Jesus on the cross in their church. He'd rather look at the map of the Toronto area. At home they have a similar map on the wall because his dad is a cab driver and he's always quizzing himself about street names and shortcuts.

During math class, Patryk goes to the side of the classroom to sharpen his pencil. Nobody's looking so he opens up the coffee tin full of pushpins. He takes a purple one and puts it carefully into the change pocket of his jeans. They're Levi's from Goodwill. His parents won't allow him and his sisters to wear acid wash jeans. Their parents say people in Poland are desperate for good Levi's, so why damage nice jeans?

For the rest of the day, every once in a while, Patryk touches the pushpin in his pocket, just to make sure it's there. Most of the time, he feels the metal tip from the side. Once in a while, he pokes the pin into his skin. Just a little bit.

At recess he looks closely at the pin. It's like a tiny top hat on a metal stick.

The pin in his pocket reminds him that he's not stuck in one place on a map. He can go *anywhere*.

***

Patryk's mother sits on the couch darning socks and keeps changing the TV channel from the game show *Definition* to the news. Next to her their father slouches and dozes. Paulina and her dolls are having a tea party. Above the sound of the TV there's a sudden screeching of fire trucks leaving the fire station at Eglinton and Warden.

Patryk and Danika sit at the kitchen table. Danika plays Scrabble with herself across from him. She turns the letters 'T-O-R-O-N-T-O' into 'NOT ROOT'. Then 'RON TOOT'. And 'NOR OTTO'. Then the best one. 'TON O ROT'. Lots of Polish words and names don't work well because they're too long with too many zeds and c's and y's.

Patryk slowly pours coins out of a pickle jar on to the tablecloth. These are all the coins the family has collected since the summer. He separates them into piles, taking out the American coins first. Their sides show pictures of men with serious faces, buildings, torches, and eagles. Queen Elizabeth is on all the rest, with more hair than the men, and a crown. Patryk picks out the loonies which first started being used in the summer. He slides all the copper maple leaves into one pile. Then the silvery beavers into another. Now he can separate the Bluenose boats from the caribous. Patryk rolls the coins into wrappers, and bunches the ends shut. Even though he's only ten, his parents trust him to do this. He doesn't know what the money will be used for. Maybe rent.

On TV, the news announcer speaks with a serious voice about a fourteen-year-old boy in Hamilton who was stabbed in the chest by someone who wanted his Sony Walkman. The injured boy is in critical condition.

"That boy is your age, Danika. You should not watch this," their mother says. But she doesn't change the channel or turn the TV off.

"It's not any worse than sports," Danika replies. "With men beating each other up. And getting paid to do it."

"Or fighting a war," Patryk says.

"Hurting is not a game," their mother says. "Or entertainment." She shifts on the couch. "Television and these videogames, so much violence and death." She puts her hand on the side of her face. "And movies full of ...," she searches for the right word. "*Reproduction?*" She laughs then sighs.

Like many evenings, Patryk imagines he's a teacher and gives everyone in his family a letter grade based on how he feels about them.

His mother can be sweet and funny, tickling him, and wagging her finger with a straight face when joking. But lately she's been crabby. *Do this, now! Don't do that. Not now. Wait.* And always letting Paulina get away with things. Everything runs on *momtime.* Buying and cooking food. Doing chores. Finishing homework. Going to church. Getting to sleep.

Earlier today he and Danika had been out shopping with her. At Loblaws their mother had said to him: "Don't correct my English!" Then, when they got home she said: "Why didn't you correct my English at K-Mart? You let me embarrass myself!" Today he gives his mother a C.

"Just change the channel," says Danika. "It's boring, anyway." She flicks her hair behind her ears. "It wouldn't be if we had cable." Their parents don't say anything as if they haven't heard her.

Danika listens more than she talks. She gives warnings like *I wouldn't do that if I were you.* Now Patryk actually likes sitting near her because she smells sweet and fruity. She seems to know just the right time to correct their mother's English. After his mom had scolded him for correcting her English, Danika hugged him. He'd give Danika an *A* today.

Dad grumbles in his sleep on the couch. As usual he's tired from driving, and he helps a friend do home renovations on weekends. Two nights a week he's also taking night courses to get his engineering license in Canada. Lately, he tickles and teases Patryk less. Once in a while, his dad wants to be all friendly, and pulls Patryk close to him and kisses his head, as if he's a little baby. But usually his father's words are filled with sharp blasts of cold air and the word *up. Grow up. Hurry up. Shut up!* He would give his dad a *D* today for sure.

Paulina is better than usual. Today she's barely sucked her thumb and cried. When she stuck out her tongue at him, and he made scissors with his fingers like he was going to cut it off, she just laughed instead of whining and running to their mom or dad. She is only four after all. He'd give her a *B*.

Patryk is happiest at home when they're sitting like this and no one is talking except someone on TV. Then he doesn't *have to* listen.

***

A few days later, the classroom activity of putting the pushpins on the world map gets complicated. Marcus doesn't know where his dad was born or even if his dad is still alive. Cindy needs more pins than everyone else because she was born in northern Ontario and then adopted by parents born in Scarborough. Other kids have step- and half-brothers and sisters. Ms. Cowan has to get more pushpins.

***

On Friday night Patryk lies in bed trying to fall asleep. The rumbling of buses on the street and the voices of his parents in the kitchen keep him awake.

His mother says she'd like to train as a pharmacist. Paulina is still too young, his father says. They should save up to move to downtown Toronto where he might be able to get a better job.

His mother's voice starts to hiss, like a kettle just starting to whistle. Then there's the horse-like neighing of his father clearing his throat. They start to argue. His mother talks in a sing-song voice. Patryk pictures her faking a smile, bobbing her head side to side. She's making fun of their father who forces out a fake laugh. Then he yells something and her first name: "Joanna!"

"Quiet, Fryderyk!" she says in a softer voice.

His father says something else in a harsh whisper. Then the apartment front door is opened and closed, not loudly but noticeably. His father must be going out for a walk or a drive, and maybe a drink of beer.

On nights like this Patryk used to get up to go to his mother and give her a hug. But he just wants to sleep.

Paulina starts crying in the bedroom she shares with Danika. Their mom goes to comfort her. He knows that later their mother will stay up late talking to Danika.

His father always says Canada has too many different kinds of people with too many languages and cultures. And he says that's why people don't understand each other here. In Poland, everyone speaks one language and understands each other, he says.

As Danika would say: *Yeah right, dad.*

***

Sunday morning Patryk wakes up still feeling a little bit sick from too much candy from Halloween the night before. He had been a decent Spiderman. Danika had dressed up as much like Madonna as she could get away with, and Paulina had been a bunny.

Instead of getting up and getting ready to go to church, their father sleeps in. He's an atheist and doesn't see the use of church. On the other hand, their mother sees the value in meeting different people, and some days she believes in God. Patryk isn't quite sure what to think. Praying seems like saying the words of a national anthem like O Canada. It's like pledging your allegiance to heaven, which is a country that might exist and that you might get to go to when you die.

Danika doesn't mind going to church. She flirts with boys there even though she says they're mostly losers. Her hair is fluffy and sticky like Silly String. And she wears makeup and a dress. Their mom looks like a Polish version of Lady Diana with her blonde hair parted in the middle. Even her shoulders are fluffed up by the shoulder pads in her dress. Paulina runs around with the other kids. Some of them are even wearing their Halloween costumes from last night.

It's November 1st and in Poland it's All Saints Day, for remembering people who died. Some of the adults look sad and serious. Being at church on Sundays is the only time Patryk wonders what it would have been like to have stayed in Poland. He can't remember living there. They had left in 1978 when he was just a one-year-old baby. They went from Warsaw north to Gdańsk and took a boat to Denmark. His parents say they wanted to get out to make a better life for their children.

If they were in Poland he could see his grandmother. Danika says she's really sweet and that when they left she had cried like someone died. Sometimes Patryk and Danika talk with her on the phone, but only once every month or two. It's hard to arrange a time to call her and it costs a lot. Their grandmother has to go to the house of a friend of a friend. And usually their mom hogs the phone anyway. Patryk can talk Polish pretty well with his parents, but it's hard to talk with his grandmother. The words she uses are so fast, and some are different from the ones he knows.

In the basement of the church there are usually Polish lessons after the service, but not today because it's All Saints Day. When Patryk goes downstairs to use the washroom he sees the map of Poland on the wall. He can't decide if it's shaped more like a crispy potato pancake or a pork *sznycel*. Poland looks trapped between East Germany, Czechoslovakia, the USSR, and the Baltic Sea. Patryk thinks of putting the purple pushpin on the map but it would look so out of place.

***

On the field trip at the top of the CN tower, Ms. Cowan and the rest of the class are listening to the tour guide. Snow has frosted the buildings down below. Toy cars and people slowly move in straight lines along the streets and sidewalks.

Patryk looks to Scarborough in the east. Everyone in his family is out there, somewhere. Paulina is at daycare in the church basement. Danika is in school, probably flirting with some boy. His father is driving his cab through slush. At the pharmacy where she works, his mother is punching numbers on the cash register.

Part of Patryk wishes his family was here with him, and part of him is glad they aren't. He looks toward Lake Ontario and up at the gray clouds. He feels weighed down and weightless at the same time, like an astronaut. No one is looking so he quickly takes the pin out of his pocket and scratches 'Patryk was here' on the window ledge.

AGAVE AMERICANA

Eva Stachniak

AGAVE, **MAGDA READS** aloud, the shrill of her Polish consonants still betraying her after twenty-two years in Canada, *is monocarpic. For years it doesn't do much, but grows, until, without any apparent reason, it sprouts a shower of bright-yellow flowers. Only then its giant leaves lose their elasticity, its skin wrinkles, and it withers.*

"No kidding, Ma," Kate says, frowning, suspicious of what her librarian mother would dig out next. (The frown should've gone the way of all the other accoutrements of adolescence but didn't.) Patting her very pregnant belly. Inside that growing protrusion is Magda's first grandchild.

Never mind, book closed. (*Plants for the Future,* new library acquisition, still to be catalogued.) *Agave americana* is just something to talk about on Kate's first day home. Innocuous and yet not altogether trivial.

Kate, twenty-six, is back with her for the summer. Pregnant, alone. Not *really* alone, Magda corrects herself for there's a husband, a home in far away Timmins and, here in Toronto, a whole army of girlfriends who will soon, too soon, claim her daughter's attention. The husband, Jamie, has just started a wedding video business and had to stay in Timmins. Magda would like to warn Kate not to be flippant about such separations. Remind her how insidious they can become. How much energy will have to be wasted on being together again, even in the marital bed where room needs to be made for this other, hot, fidgety, snoring, teeth-grinding body. She won't, though. Her business is to accept Kate the way she is. Not quite alone, fully pregnant, fascinated by that new life inside her, her own stretching skin. Exposing it freely, with pride.

Magda is fifty-two. People still describe her as an attractive woman. Finely chiselled (although she thinks herself too bony), graceful, with a knack for adornment. Able to spot an Art Deco necklace in a garage sale trinket box, a chic jacket at a vintage store. She was twenty-six when Kate was born; she likes the symmetry of numbers that have spread them through time.

This very morning, right after Kate's arrival and a flurry of unpacking, Magda found a cocoa-butter stick on the bathroom counter —*excellent at preventing stretch marks*—and a bottle of *prenatal and post-partum* vitamins. She took one. Swallowed the pill without water, and she can still feel its hard shape in her throat.

Kate, Magda thinks, is one of these rare women who truly like their bodies. This is a thought of awe, envy almost. Once when Kate was about seven, Magda found her naked in bed, running her hand over her flat chest and then licking it. "Yummy," she said when Magda asked her what she tasted like, trying not to look at the hairless skin of her private parts. This was an expression Kate brought from her Canadian school. *"Private parts,"* she said when Magda began washing her there one day, as she had always done, her voice so fiercely firm. "Don't touch."

"Only seventy-five per cent chance for a girl," Kate says now. "The cord was between her legs. She can still be a boy."

The grammar of that last sentence makes Magda laugh, but she accepts its internal logic. Deep down she knows it's a girl. The way she knew when Kate was inside her, kicking her with her still only imagined but already real heel.

Kate will be in Toronto for two months, then Jamie will come and they'll go to visit his parents, in Owen Sound. Magda will go to Timmins for a month after the delivery. Now Kate is sitting at the table in Magda's condo. Two bedrooms and a den. Magda bought it seven years ago after Yanush—Kate's father—told her he wasn't coming back. They had their problems before, but nothing that would justify the abruptness and the finality of his desertion. He went back to Poland to gather material for a series of interviews on the first decade of the post-communist transformation. Lined up writers, academics, former and current politicians and dissidents. Everyone he wanted to talk to agreed. "It was incredible," Yanush told her on that dreary November day of 2000, after he had interviewed Michnik himself, but then said nothing when Magda complained how empty the house felt and how much Kate missed him. Stupidly she also kept asking for some Warsaw gossip. Who came back, who was planning to leave.

"I've met someone," Yanush said.

The way the Toronto real estate is now, Magda wouldn't be able to afford the house they had sold then. A semi in Bloor West Village. A crab-apple tree in the front, lavish profusion of pink flowers every spring. Their first real Canadian home, bought as soon as Magda got her library job. A scene for Kate's most daring feats, promises of what, in Polish, Magda calls *polot,* daredevil's courage mixed with grace. Magda still smiles at the memory of the phone call she received from the principal's office when Kate was twelve. "Your daughter is dancing on the roof of your house. The whole school has gone to watch her!"

Where is this Kate now? The Kate who wanted to trek through Australia, climb mountains in Nepal? Took scuba-diving and rock-climbing lessons? The daughter who once danced on the roof dropped out of university. Since then she's been a telemarketer, a counsellor at a summer camp, and a life guard at YMCA where she met Jamie. Magda thought him an improvement over a series of pimply boyfriends who never managed to mumble more than: "Hello, Mrs. Topolski." Jamie ran survival courses in the Ontario wilderness and on the very first day Kate brought him home lectured Magda on what he called the basic fives: Five minutes without air, five days without water, five weeks without food. This is what Magda should always remember and take into account, Jamie said, the limits of human endurance. She forced herself to ignore his shapeless khaki pants that kept slipping when he bent, revealing white hairy skin. *Bum cleavage,* another of the expressions Kate once taught Magda.

Kate must've sensed her thoughts then, for she frowned and left for the kitchen to fetch more beer. And Jamie kept talking: "Remember that the city has dulled your senses, and this is why you cannot fully trust yourself. One of your sides is always heavier. When you're walking alone in the woods, this heavier side pulls you in one direction and you walk in circles."

By now the wilderness school has gone belly up, and Jamie is a wedding video producer. Last time Magda saw him he had put on weight (must be all this beer drunk straight from the bottle) and pontificated on the importance of capturing precious memories. Making them last.

"If it's a girl," Kate says, "Jamie wants to call her Janet. If it's a boy, I'll name him Patrick."

What is Magda supposed to say? Forget that Janet Sullivan is Jamie's mother? Offer more trivia about the Agave?

"Have you talked to your father recently?" Magda asks.

Kate stretches her arms and shakes her head. She went to Warsaw once but didn't say much either of Yanush or his new wife (ten years younger than Magda) when she returned. Other than saying that her father hasn't changed much, which could mean anything, good or bad. "We had to hire a new camera-man," Kate says now. Her hair is almost white, a lovely contrast with her tanned skin. "Seven weddings in June alone."

"That's encouraging," Magda says and takes out eggs from the fridge. She will scramble them, the way Kate has always liked. Set, not runny.

In Poland, before they left for Canada, Yanush was a journalist. And so was Magda. When the strikes in Gdańsk began, they started their own newsletter. Reported on local protests, interviewed Solidarity activists. In December of 1981 they were both arrested but told they could go free, if they signed a loyalty statement. Yanush refused and was interned. Magda signed and was let go. She believed that Kate who was still called Kasia then, five months old, needed her more than Poland did. That she, Magda, had made a sacrifice, for which Kate would repay her manifold by using the opportunities her mother never had. This thought kept Magda sane in the dark months of the martial law when Yanush was still in the internment camp and many of their old friends declared her a traitor. Looked another way when they saw her in the street, pushing the pram. Or crossed to the other side and hurried away.

Was this shunning the reason why Yanush agreed to leave for Canada? Not for Kate's sake, or Magda's, though. Whatever he did, Yanush did for himself. Looking at how little his daughter has done with her life, he may've been right.

Don't, Magda tells herself firmly, as she cracks four eggs into a measuring cup, adds a tablespoon of milk and whips it all up with a fork. *Don't go that route. She is your only child. Still young. Still untried.*

Cranberry juice for Kate, but Magda pours herself a glass of white wine and takes a sip as the egg mixture slowly sets in a buttered frying pan. She won't think of Yanush who has a whole new family (his son has just turned three), and a prestigious job in Warsaw's *Polityka*. Who calls Canada *the land of philistines, of made-up problems, a land paralyzed with self-satisfied delusions.* He doesn't regret his eighteen years of exile there, precisely because they made him see with acute clarity what really mattered to him.

Obviously that something didn't include Magda or Kate.

Kate tries a forkful of eggs, gags, and pushes the plate away. But she drinks the juice and eats all the strawberries from the ceramic bowl, the one with a yellow fish on the bottom. As strawberries disappear the fish becomes more and more prominent, its funny looking blue eye staring at Magda, warning her not to get too wrapped up in Kate, in Yanush, and (most of all) in the thoughts of Paul, her lover.

Only yesterday (unreal already, separated by Kate's solid and pregnant presence) Magda covered herself with a sheet, her neck reddened from Paul's kisses. This skin of hers, drying up so fast, itching from all that friction. This body deformed by time. Her right foot growing a bunion from all the cheap shoes she had worn. The stretch marks from having Kate without the benefit of cocoa butter and pre-natal vitamins. These small unexplainable flaps of flesh that grow on her arms, harmless but irritating in their useless, pigheaded persistence.

"Now what?" she had asked.

He laughed and kissed her on her chapped, dry lips and this memory alone makes her long for him now, a dull throb lodged in her belly. Like hunger pain this pain of absence.

"Mama," Kate says. "You aren't listening."

There's a new note in Kate's voice. A plea? Another challenge?

Magda picks a fork and eats some of the scrambled eggs, now cold, in need of more salt. Drinks another sip of wine.

Four weeks ago Paul Walker was one of the presenters in the series Magda's library branch runs every first Wednesday of the month: *Creating an effective resume*. (Ever since a local poet drew the total of three people, her supervisor urged her to try less literary topics.) The attendance had been excellent. Forty-five participants, teenagers too, in gym clothes and baseball caps, listening in rapt concentration.

Magda and Paul talked briefly afterwards, in the library room where Magda had prepared a small display of self-help books: *Little Gold Book of YES!, How to Improve your Life, Luck, and Career*. Paul complimented her on the way she tied her scarf. (Very Parisian, he had said.) She told him he was an excellent speaker (which he was). Two days later he called her at the library and asked her out to dinner. She can still see the thin curve of Paul's smile from that evening when his knee touched hers under the table. And his tongue moistening the cracked skin.

"I'll check my e-mails," Kate announces (her chin stained red from the last of the strawberries) and goes to the den where Magda keeps her computer. From the back her daughter looks unchanged, though more sluggish and wobbly. Soon, very soon the phone will ring (it's a surprise it hasn't already) and Kate will be off with one of her girlfriends who are now teachers, medical interns, lawyers. Dot, the most beloved, is doing a PhD at McGill. "In social psychology," Kate says, without the slightest shadow of unease.

Kate doesn't know about Paul, or others before him. She doesn't know of her mother's lust, thick and sticky. Feeling like a fly in tar, to use a Polish expression, awkward, tied by clingy threads that drag after her, hold her to the surface. Anticipating yet another defeat that might unhinge her this time, turn her into a thwarted witch of fairy tales.

Magda believes pregnancy should be a happy time. Blissfully self-absorbed, joyful (hers was only partially such, given the food shortages and arrests of dissident-friends). Such a pregnancy will arm the baby against the stickiness of life. She believes that by hiding her own disappointments and fears from Kate, Magda is contributing to her grand-daughter's happiness. Holding back something of the present, not to spoil the future.

This isn't the entire truth, though. Even if Kate weren't pregnant, Magda wouldn't confide in her. Tell her how, even now, Magda can feel Paul's hand digging into her hair, pressing the base of her skull. No, she would never talk of her own private—no, not parts.

Humiliations?

Hopes?

"Mama," Kate calls from the den. "Look at this." She's laughing so it cannot be bad news.

The subject line of the e-mail says: "Amazing." Third-graders somewhere in the States were asked to complete old proverbs: *Don't bite the hand that.... Better late than....* Their teacher collected the results and now an e-mail is turning up in everyone's mailbox. As chain e-mails go, this is a notch better than the ones that tell you to *send this message to five other people within five minutes* or face seven years of bad luck.

Don't bite the hand that ... looks dirty.

"This *is* funny," Magda agrees, but Kate shoots her a look of disappointment.

"Not just funny, Mama," she insists.

If you lie down with dogs, you'll ... stink in the morning.

"Will I see you again?" Paul asked yesterday, in his downtown condo. (An Ikea futon, but also an elegant brown leather sofa, a glass coffee-table with a film of dust on it. *A Hitchhiker's Guide to the Galaxy* beside his bed, its spine broken in half.) "Her ambitions lay elsewhere," was all he said about his former wife. A phantom, an apparition whose traces Magda spotted and recorded. A see-through box with false eyelashes. (A joke, Paul said laughing, a fancy dress party accessory.) A facial scrub, half-used, half-abandoned and already dried-up.

Paul lying stark naked on his crumpled bed, hands folded under his head, watching her secure the sheet around her body as she walked towards the bathroom.

When the blind lead the blind ... get out of the way.

"Mama, you aren't listening," Kate says. There is a frown on her forehead. A crease. She pulls at the skin of her cheek as she leans on her hand. A habit that'll soon translate into wrinkles. Will Kate, the goddess of her own body, really not mind? Think the wrinkles cute or immaterial?

"I *am* listening," Magda says. "Very funny."

If at first you don't succeed ... get new batteries.

This time it is Magda who laughs out loud first. Is her daughter psychic, or what? Or is this bit of childish wisdom just a pure coincidence, a gift of chance?

Kate pulls her tight t-shirt over her belly. Too short to cover even the top of it. Her belly button had been pierced once in some girlish ritual of sworn friendship. There is no stud in that little hole, now, a wound closed, its outlines still there to be reclaimed. Or forgotten.

And so they sit together, mother and daughter, on this (so rare) Sunday morning and talk. Of a baby shower Kate's girlfriends will have for her in spite of Magda's misgivings. (She still thinks it a crass custom, shameless present grabbing.) Of the good air of Timmins (compared to Toronto). They sit and talk and drink (herbal tea and more wine) until the phone does ring and Kate departs hastily, and the rest of Magda's day turns thicker, even more impossible to fathom.

***

Later, at night, Magda wakes up startled by the noise. It takes her a while to realize that Kate has returned (well past midnight, stumbling over something in the hall, and then taking a long shower).

Her head hurts from too much wine, her right leg tingles and itches. She hears Kate opening the bathroom door, dropping something on the floor. Something which gives a hard thud, but doesn't break. Going into the guest bedroom, closing the door behind her.

Magda tosses and turns for a long while, on the edge of sleep. The dream that comes catches her by surprise.

She is lying in bed, naked. The linen is snow white and old-fashioned, crisp, beautiful linen of her childhood. With lace inserts, starched, ironed, smelling of mangle steam. In this bed, time is still and lambent, bathing in the glow of the yellow streetlamp outside. Kate is bending over her, her lips moving, telling her something.

What?

But then, with dream-like logic, it all becomes clear, for—prompted by Kate's radiant smile—Magda touches her own breasts. The nipples are swollen, dripping with milk. Thick and so sweet on her fingers when she licks them.

BACHELOR

Jowita Bydlowska

THERE ARE EIGHT of us in the limo, all gowns and makeup and perfume and squealing. This reminds me of a wedding I went to last summer. The wedding was held in a barn. We rode to it, to the barn, through cornfields, in a limo, squealing just like this. There was champagne, and here we have champagne, too.

One of the girls loses one of her fake lashes and there is frantic lifting of heels until another girl says: "I'm not fucking getting my pantyhose all mucked up," and it's as if everyone came to; they all sit up and stop looking; me too. The fake lash girl starts peeling off the remaining lash.

"Let's have more fucking champagne," the eyelash girl says. Most of us are half in the bag already.

A nurse from Calgary, Trisha, is the first to get out of the limo. We squeeze our faces against the tinted window. Trisha walks in her blue gown between two cameras on trolleys. Big reflector lights make her glitter dress even more glitter.

"He's gonna go for her. First impressions."

"Not true."

"Just watch." An elbow digs hard into my ribs so I sit back; across from me is the fake lash girl who says: "I'm Gina. I'm a mess."

I shake her hand. "You look fine."

"Yeah, right," Gina says.

I text my girlfriend: *I miss you.*

Later our phones are taken away.

***

I am the last one to tumble out of the limo. The lights are blinding, the top of my gown scratches—the plastic gems are sewn in with clear fishing wire.

Tom's smile is bright, like the reflectors; like one of the reflectors is actually inside his mouth. He pulls me in for a quick hug. I haven't been hugged by a man in a long time. He smells of cologne and sweat. He is sweating under those lamps, anybody would be. He softly says: "Hi there," and a shiver runs up and down my back—that's how they describe the sensation in romance novels. I've read a few to prepare.

I giggle. Unlike many other girls I don't have a dramatic entrance and a memorable line prepared. My girlfriend said to play up my Polishness, do my hair in one of those stupid braids, wrap it around my head, maybe wear something folky with sequins and flowers. I don't think so.

He says he can't wait to get to know me. Up-close his face turns out to be evenly covered in foundation. I'm reminded of one of those fancy macaroons, the caramel one.

I walk away. I hope he's turning to look at my ass. The girls whose asses get looked at usually stay on for a while.

***

Inside the house it's a sparkling tornado, a chaos of: eyes, big teeth, jewels, big earrings. The smell of perfume and hair spray is sticky; there's the smell of nervous farts, too. We're in a cloud of sweet shit.

A girl runs around and high-fives everyone, shouting: "I'm Lucy! The future Mrs. Taylor!" in between bouts of laughter. She has lost her mind already.

A girl spills some of the champagne onto another girl's dress. The cameras like four giant insects zoom in. Under their glass eyes, the girls flare. The brunette says: "What the hell is wrong with you?" to the blonde who says: "Watch it. Watch your mouth."

I empty my champagne flute. I immediately pour myself another one. Everyone sounds louder now, the alcohol increases the volume of madness. Another glass.

I read about that, how all *The Bachelor* girls are plied with food and alcohol. Everyone is drunk all the time, everyone cries. I want to cry already. I'm drunk. I'm in love with Tom Taylor. He's such an amazing guy. There were butterflies in my stomach when our eyes locked. I'm saying this or I'm thinking this or others are saying this. I can't tell. I, too, have lost my mind.

There's a stack of red roses on a table; everyone keeps glancing at it, the roses, then back like it's no big deal. I hiccup to a girl next to me—possibly a kindergarten teacher from St. John's, possibly a librarian from Victoria, I can't tell which with my drunken eyes—that the stack makes me think of when they burned witches.

"How do you mean?"

"Like when would tie a witch to a stake. But it's roses instead of wood."

She raises her eyebrow. I burst out laughing at this, at the theatricality of it.

Later I get a rose and I do everything I can to hold the burp that wants to come up as I tell Tom Taylor, yes, when he asks if I accept this rose.

***

I share room with two girls, Mandy, and June. June isn't sure if she's in love with Tom. Everyone else is almost sure now.

Tonight, we're going on a group date. This time we don't have to play beach volleyball or learn a dumb dance from the locals. We're going on a boat to look at sharks. Earlier, we were filmed opening boxes with bikinis. I got one that's lime green to go with my red hair.

June's bikini is pink. She puts it on now and does a little cat-walk for me and Mandy. June wears no makeup; her dark hair is un-ironed. Her skin looks as if it would smell of chocolate; she has dimples in her cheeks. She's only 20. She shouldn't be here among these desperados. (Yesterday she was filmed following one of the Ashleys who ran out of the gazebo crying loudly after Tom made out with another girl. June put her hand against the eye of the camera and said, "Please," softly as if she was taming an animal. The camera retreated. June put her arms around the Ashley who buried her head in June's shoulder. When June looked up, her face was a child's face.)

***

Once the boat stops, Tom reveals the surprise. We're not going to be just watching the sharks. We're going to be swimming with the sharks!

The girls shriek and jump with hands at their mouths. The sharks are visible in the water, shadows circling.

Tom takes off his shirt. The girls hoot. He's got a nice body; he's a hairless Ken. He jumps in. The sharks do nothing about it.

The girls scream some more and plead and erupt in short, crazed bursts of laughter.

Tom laughs too. "Your turn, ladies!"

"No way, no way, no way," Gina or someone who looks like her says. But one after another, the girls climb down. I don't. Tom is shouting for me to not be afraid.

For whatever reason, I'm thinking of my girlfriend becoming obsessed with a woman named Kristine. Kristine calling me and telling me about it, asking me to tell my girlfriend to leave her alone. I never told my girlfriend. I was mortified, embarrassed for both of us. Anyway, that's what I think about as I finally jump in. I put on my mask, the snorkel. I watch the sharks swim silently below me. The girls splash around but soon most of them leave the water, climb back onto the boat. There's a strange calm that spreads all over my body, liquefies it. I hold my breath.

In my head I have an image of my girlfriend's snarlmouth that says: Sometimes I fantasize about you being dead.

What?

Everyone fantasizes about their partner being dead.

I don't.

Yes you do, Daria. But only I have the balls to say it.

***

The sharks seem too close. They are not. I take a breath. They are not; they are the same distance. I surface.

"Daria," Tom shouts and waves at me. June is beside him. She smiles and waves too. "Come, Daria!" The way they are, floating there together, it makes me feel as if I would interrupt something private were I to join them.

"That's okay," I say and swim up to the boat.

On the boat, the other girls are pointing to Tom and June swimming with their heads under the surface. Their hands are touching.

A girl, Ashley or Trish, says: "She must be really desperate."

June's long dark hair is like seaweed, above her. Her moves are unhurried. I imagine Tom's watching her watching the sharks. That's what I would do.

***

I can't read Tom. I can't explain it but it's like he's teary, wet, like the tip of his nose is wet or maybe it's something in the eyes. He's got kissy eyes. I feel tense when he talks to me but not because I think of fucking him.

We only have two short conversations; both of them get interrupted by other girls. Like now: "Is it okay if I steal him for a minute?"

"Sure. Knock yourself out."

***

Later in the Crying Room, on camera, the producer asks about my frustrations.

"What should I say?"

"Why it made you upset?"

"I want my phone back. I need to text my friend."

"We can't. It's in the contract."

"Just one text."

"One text." She rolls her eyes at me. I roll my eyes back. Later I will find out that me rolling my eyes has made it into the footage.

I text both my girlfriend and my thesis supervisor: *Things are going really well!*

None of us expected that a dyke would make it past the second episode. I have more material for my paper than we hoped for.

"Okay," I say to the producer. I stare into the black eye of the camera.

"Why did you get upset with Tina stealing Tom away?"

I imagine Tom is my girlfriend. I imagine Kristine kissing my girlfriend. Fucking bitch.

"Because that was rude. I feel like Tom and I have a real connection and people keep interrupting us."

"How does Tom make you feel?"

"I'm like totally falling for him."

The camera waits.

"I can see our future together." This is something someone said on one of the episodes of *The Bachelor* I watched to prepare.

After the interview, I go and smoke behind the gazebo. It's the only place where the cameras can't get to or haven't thought of getting to.

I want to go home.

***

Tom and I get to talk for a bit longer on a group date with two other women. First, we ride horses, the cameras on trolleys, next to us. Ashley #2 shouts to the camera: "I've never been on a horse, this is amazing."

After we dismount, Tom suggests he and I go for a walk. A camera follows us, silently.

"It's like something out of Cronenberg, isn't it? Those cameras," I say to Tom.

He laughs. "Cronenberg."

I know this shit will get edited. They'll just leave the parts where we go on about our feelings.

"Who's your hero?" Tom asks. He constantly asks us, the girls, questions like that—questions that require big answers, some kind of profound confessions:

My mother who died when I was five years old.

Oh, that's terrible—cut to Tom in the Crying Room, saying to the camera, *I felt she really opened up to me, finally.*

Anyway, that's not how our conversation goes. My mother isn't dead and she's no hero. She's a narcissistic bitch. I make up a teacher. Someone who inspired me to pursue my dreams of becoming "the person I am today," maybe the Robin Williams character from *The Dead Poets Society.* I describe him, Robin Williams.

Tom says: "Wow. He really does seem like an amazing person."

***

June and I sit on the balcony. The Ocean is ink black. There's music coming from the beach bar downstairs, something bouncy.

June says: "I've never been anywhere outside of Ontario. Actually, when my mom was pregnant with me, she went to Cuba so I went to Cuba, technically." She laughs and I laugh too but only because she's laughing.

"Would you move to Montreal? With Tom?" I say.

"Yeah. Probably."

Besides me and a stand-up comedian named Kate—who I suspect is here to get exposure—for other women Tom seems to be the answer to it all. The women behave as predicted. For my thesis I argue that despite its artificial conditions *The Bachelor* mirrors the truth about how contemporary, desirable (money, looks or both) males have limitless choices: limitless number of women they get to eliminate for no reason at all or the tiniest infraction such as a show of too much emotion. In such elevated heteronormative approximation of a society, the ideals of feminism—or even something much simpler such as solidarity between women—are destroyed. But it's not regressing, I argue. It's possible that feminism is essentially destructive to the human race—abortion, birth control, equal rights —and the behaviours observed on *The Bachelor,* however troubling, are the perfect illustration of species survival: women offering themselves to one superior (money, looks or both) male specimen that is capable of impregnating them. Whether that's right or wrong is irrelevant. Biology doesn't care about integrity.

"Would you?" June says.

"What?"

"Move with Tom to Montreal?"

As soon as she says it, it occurs to me that I'm done here. *Move with Tom to Montreal.* What? Absurd.

"Why not?" she says.

I look away. "I don't feel the connection. And it was dumb to come here. It's a dumb thing to do. To be here."

"You really think that."

"Yeah. You could leave, too. You could do so much better," I say. It just comes out. "You could go to school, travel—"

"You trying to rescue me?" She doesn't say it rudely. It's a rude thing to say but the way she says it, it's more wistful than anything else.

"No. You're not an idiot, but you don't need him to rescue you either."

She says nothing for a moment. Then her words, measured as if this was a line in a movie: "I live in a small town with a wetbrain father who's drinking himself to death and I cannot leave him because what will people say. *This* way I can leave."

"Okay. Got it." I suppose I feel something like relief. I'd rather she'd be a liar than an idiot. But I still don't know what to wish her: to win or to lose.

***

Later, after I pack—and after I talk on camera in the Crying Room about how I don't feel the connection and blah blah blah—June walks me out the side door. The beach bar is closed; now there's only a sound of cicadas, quiet talk and giggling on balconies above us.

We hug. "Good luck," I say, letting go of her strong and soft body.

Her face looks almost feral in the half shadow. "To you, too," she says.

I walk around to the front of the hotel.

***

The makeup artist fluffs my hair, powders my nose. "If you're going to cry, make sure to dab a corner in your eyes so it doesn't smudge your mascara," she says and hands me a Kleenex.

Before the limo shows up (the camera eyes trained on the driveway already), I go behind the gazebo to smoke.

"Hey," a voice says somewhere in the darkness behind me.

I turn around. Tom. Hiding in the bushes, smoking too. He looks different. Older. Tired.

"Hey."

"I'm sorry you feel that way. I don't want you to go," he says. He's reciting lines. With no cameras on him, he's still reciting lines.

"It's okay. No need to. Nobody's watching," I say.

He says nothing.

"I have to go. I'm sorry. I'm here for the wrong reasons. I'm writing a paper. For my thesis. About the show," I say. His lying, prompts my honesty.

He exhales. "What?"

"Don't rat me out."

"Seriously. What the fuck."

I haven't heard him swear before. Or seen him smoke.

I say: "I'm really sorry."

He says nothing for a long time. Then: "I wish I could do the same."

"What?"

"Leave." He points to the driveway with his chin.

"Leave?"

"Yeah. Don't rat *me* out. I like June. I knew it right away as soon as I met her. Now I'm just going through the motions. But those girls. I feel badly. I'm a jerk. I was never a jerk and now I'm a jerk."

"You're not a jerk," I say but think: you are a total jerk. Only a jerk would think this is a good idea, to come on this show where women humiliate themselves like that. For you. Jerk. But it doesn't matter. I'm just writing a paper on jerks. And girls who want to be with jerks. All the girls in that hotel, dreaming, planning ... getting shitfaced out of anxiety. Ashleys crying in the toilet, Trisha burning Gina's hair on purpose with the straightener, Lisa throwing up in the bathroom after binge-eating a bag of cookies. He'll pick June. Of course, he'll pick June. June with her chocolate skin and eyes, her fresh face. Her symmetry. Twenty years old. Biology.

"This show has made a monster out of me," he says

"Don't be a fucking drama queen. It's okay. The heart wants what it wants, right?"

He exhales. He says: "Exactly. And it wants June."

"There you go."

"It's so good to tell someone. Thank you," he says and stubs out a cigarette. Five minutes later he hugs me in front of the idling limo. I cling onto to him a little too hard. His body shifts, gently, arms letting go of my waist; the camera films us looking into each other's eyes. I dab the corner of the Kleenex in my eyes, careful not to smudge. In the limo I pull out my phone to text my girlfriend but I don't text her; I don't know what to text.

LESSONS IN TRANSLATION

Kasia Jaronczyk

I'VE ALWAYS BEEN a translator. The pages of my life have been written in many languages, adapted to new contexts, and re-interpreted with every transition. Translation means "moving across," and I've carried different versions of myself, like calques, through all boundaries, real and imagined. My roots were torn out like baby teeth, but my etymology has survived. In my words are the sememes of my existence.

The source text

When I was little, I lived in a house with so many windows and doors that I often lost my way and travelled through rooms until my mother found me and cried out my name with the joy of a writer who has found *le mot juste*. A succession of governesses taught me to translate passages from Polish into English, French, German and Italian.

On my tenth birthday I received a baby deer whom I named Albert. I kept him in our garden and fed him milk from my old baby bottle. He licked my fingers with his tongue, rough like tree bark. He told me that he was happy and that he loved me.

On my twelfth birthday my father gave me a typewriter, which I used to write Albert's biography and plays in different languages, which my cousins acted out during family gatherings.

When soldiers came, followed by crowds of peasants, they seized my father's textile factory, and occupied our house. They stole vegetables and fruit from our garden, fought over the sausages and preserves with our identical twin cooks Anna and Hanna, until the sisters disappeared one night amidst shouting and shooting. In the morning my mother sat at the kitchen table and cried, cradling the rolling pin, which was still covered with flour. The front of her dress stayed white for the entire day. Her footprints, floury halos on the mahogany floors, were the prints of ghosts.

When the soldiers had eaten all the food, they shot Albert and ate him.

New context

We were told that nothing belonged to us anymore. The soldiers trampled through our house, slashed the paintings, wounded the furniture and murdered the grand piano.

In our library emptied of books, which the solders used to build fires, I asked my father, as I stuffed his money in my underwear: "Why do the soldiers call us thieves when we can buy anything we want?" I could hear the stomping of their boots outside the door. My father laughed and choked on my mother's rings, which he had been gulping like candy. Tears ran down his face

"What is morally bankrupt?" I asked about the words I'd learned from the soldiers. I already knew that "common property" meant that all our things were taken away, "a tyrant" was someone who had a large house and owned a factory, and "the people" were everybody but us.

Our servants took our linen, pots and pans, cutlery and candlesticks. They even stole my dolls. The names they used to call us, *Pan, Pani, Panienko*, sounded like insults when they paraded in front of us in our "bourgeois clothes" and my mother's make-up smeared on their faces like a mask.

At first I thought it was a game whose rules I asked them to explain. I grabbed my nanny's hand and said: "Tell the soldiers that you are happy here and that you love me." She ripped my necklace off and pushed me down on the newly bare floor.

There are some words that don't have to be translated, like mama and papa, and some words are never enough, like love or happiness, hot and cold, and pain.

Translation

In Siberia we lived in a one-room cabin, with grass stuffed into the blowing spaces between the logs. When we were marched to the camp, I was amazed at the bleakness of the landscape—dark trees marking the snow like runes. But soon all I could think about was the pain of frozen hands and feet, and frost-bitten faces. Tree trunks were prison bars and beyond them was freedom to die in the never-ending winter. The long walk made me feel light-headed, transparent. When I sank in the snow I felt I was translated bodily, like the Virgin Mary to Heaven, and the snow became clouds. My father carried me. His hands, once white and slender on piano keys, grew stigmata from where the handle of the axe rubbed against his skin, before the wounds changed into calluses.

My mother and I picked roots and moss when we ran out of food. Hunger. You cannot know the nullifying meaning of that word till you experience it. The hollowness that reaches into bones. In your brain lodges a single, uninterrupted thought, splinter sharp even through sleep. The wanting that makes you steal from your own mother. When I stuffed a handful of dried-out berries from my mother's basket into my mouth, she slapped me. The juice ran out the corners of my mouth mixed with blood. I wiped it with my hand and licked my palm clean. My mother cried.

Equivalent text

How does one learn the importance of words? When does understanding what another person says become more powerful than prayer?

A Russian guard ambushed us at our family prayer, because God does not exist in a communist country. I felt the cold ring of a gun barrel against the back of my head. I heard the soldier shout something I couldn't understand. I wished I could say to him, in the language of his mother: "Don't kill me."

If I could tell him about myself, he would know me. Then he couldn't hate me.

I didn't know that he was joking, that he laughed with his comrades behind my back and shot into the air.

Gunshots sound the same in every language.

Foreignization

I asked one of the local women to teach me Russian in exchange for work. As I washed her floors I learned words that I hoped would save us. How was it possible that people who shared so many words with us could hate us and call us enemies?

When the British came, we thought that we were saved, but they sent us farther away from Poland, into a land inhabited by strange people and more unfamiliar than Siberia—Tanganyika.

We have a word in Polish, tęsknota, which is an emotion more powerful than longing, it is more like missing something, like nostalgia for a thing, person or place lost or taken from one's life.

As we passed through the ascetic landscapes of Iran and Palestine, I was thirsty for the minds of people who lived there. I wanted to enter their thoughts, to learn about everything I saw and name it in their language.

Paraphrase

When, as a child, I thought of Africa, I saw deserts where camels' humps rose over sand dunes; forests where monkeys hung on branches like hairy fruit; grassy plains with trees whose tops were flattened by the weight of the sky, into which giraffes reached out their crane necks, and where elephants and lions fought for supremacy. These fantastic landscapes were populated by naked black people with lives so different from my own that they were unimaginable.

But the village in Tanganyika, with its thatched mud huts,

narrow paths made by feet that left prints identical to ours, was the same as villages in Poland. We heard the hens' familiar cries, and the flies buzzed over the food in the same way; the food, although different, tasted just as good at the end of the day as a treasured family recipe. In the morning the farmers milked the cows and fed the chickens. They worked in the fields till nightfall, just like peasants in Poland.

And so we became farmers for the British. We worked with the natives under a sky so hot that I missed Siberia. Even if I knew how to speak the language of this new country, I wouldn't know how to make the people understand what winter was, or cold, or snow. My mother told me they didn't have the words for it. I wondered if there were any languages, any nations that didn't have words for hate, or war, or kill.

Back translation

Our lives were translated again.

At Christmastime I sat at dinner at Lord Delamere's house, whose land we worked, and stared at the roasted goose in front of me. In Poland we were allowed to eat only fish at Christmas Eve.

"What are the holidays like in your ...?" Lady Delamere asked me, but she seemed to have dropped her words on the floor along with her fork when I shook Ajabu's hand, foreign to me in a white glove, when he served me bread sauce. Ajabu and I used to hunt for stray hens' eggs together when we were little.

Target language

I learned a new language, Swahili, and grew to love it. It is a language that cannot be foreign to anyone because it has no true native speakers—it isn't affiliated to any ethnicity, so either it is a foreign language to everyone, or everyone can be its native speaker. It is an all-inclusive language, like a large house. I could recognize a lot of words that were German, English and French in it. It reflects the love its people have for words and for the things they describe. The preponderance of diminutive forms.

Adaptation

"Tanganyika" is composed of two Swahili words: "tanga," which means sail, and "nyika," which means uninhabited plain or wilderness. And it is how I felt when I lived there: as if I were sailing through wilderness. I was slowly finding myself there, learning and translating the Swahili names of local plants and insects, the different peoples who lived there, and their names for me. I wanted to learn Swahili so well that I would think and dream in it.

Tanganyika later became a part of Tanzania. "Tanzania" was another miraculous word. A word born of the fusion of two distinct words: "Tanganyika" and "Zanzibar." A portmanteau word. For portmanteau people.

Fidelity

My child was a portmanteau child. His father was Ajabu.

Ajabu was beautiful. The darkness of his skin was so deep that it had no surface: I could plunge my hands into him as into water. The redness of his mouth and tongue, the orange of his open palms, glowed like embers I extinguished with my body.

We lived in our own world. When we made love we spoke in our own tongues. We didn't need to translate anything; we knew what we meant from the sounds alone.

I want you, I love you.

I need you.

Is she from your village?

Don't leave me.

Don't take away my son.

***

I ran away to the capital city, Dar es Salaam (which means House of Peace) with my son. My lover stayed in his village and married a woman his mother chose for him. I worked at a cosmetic counter in a large department store, a Babel Tower, through which crowds of people passed daily in search of fulfillment. I knew what they wanted and sold it to them in their own languages: what they considered better versions of themselves.

Soon we had to move again. Every shadow behind me looked like Ajabu reaching for our son. My parents decided to go back to Poland; they were too old to translate their life again, in some new place. They longed to be back even if it meant living under the communist rule. I chose to go to Canada, an amalgam country, like a compound word.

Transparency

With my son I found happiness. We communicated without words. I knew when he was hungry or needed to be changed; when he wanted to know that I was there. I could feel his emotions without having to name them. He called me without using words, without saying my name.

When I had carried him inside me, I spoke to him in my thoughts and aloud in my mother tongue and in his father's. He spoke to me from the inside of me, saying "I am here", and I knew I was pregnant before my body revealed it to me.

As he grew older, I wanted to protect our connectedness for as long as I could. I built our own language, a home made of sounds. We had special pet names for favourite objects, places and foods; for feelings and caresses that we shared; for toys and games we played.

But when he went to school, no one could understand him. My son named an object on a picture card in our made-up language and was told that he was wrong. Other children laughed at him. He cried when he came home. So we spoke our language less and less.

Metaphrase

I became a translator and worked in a lawyer's office to help new immigrants. Now I work as a government interpreter. My job is to translate exactly what politicians say. I can predict what words are going to be spoken next and I decide how sentences are going to end.

Glossary:

Back-translation—translation of a text back into the language of the original.

Calque—a word or phrase borrowed from another language by literal translation.

Fidelity—the extent to which a translation accurately renders the meaning of the source text.

Foreignization—translation that resists contemporary cultural and stylistic features of the target language in order to convey the total impact of the source text.

Metaphrase—literal translation.

Paraphrase—conveys the content of a source text at the expense of literality.

Portmanteau word—combining of two (or more) words and their meanings into one new word.

Sememe—primary denotation.

Transparency—the degree to which a translation appears to a native speaker of the target language to have been written in that language.

THE BEAR

Katarzyna Jaśkiewicz

SHE DID NOT pitch up her tent on the usual spot. The place was promised to her but when she came, she found the meadow filled with cars and tents. She had to content herself with the spot in the woods close to the lodge, gripped by two roads, like pliers. She never liked that place, and always felt pity for those who pitched their tents there. For her the only place for a tent was on the wide meadow. Once, she sat there in a pouring rain watching a prairie dog feed on puffy clover heads. On the meadow she listened to birds and felt like she was just about to touch something that she missed all her life. What could be touched in the woods between two roads? What could be seen there?

Of course later, when the bear came, the location of her tent next to the lodge proved to be safer, and those camping on the meadow escaped first. But on the day of her arrival, she built her camp feeling deceived. First, she put up the tent. Then, the kitchen tent. She dragged a wooden table and placed it inside. She found a small ladder in the garage behind the lodge, and used it to attach a rope between two trees, and pulled a tarp over it. Then, she went around, placing poles under the tarp, creating the cover for both tents, a veranda-like space between them. The sky was overcast when she was bringing a mattress, a sleeping bag, a cooler and other bags from the car, but when it finally started to pour, everything was ready. She sat in front of the tent with a freshly brewed mug of tea, listening to the rain, thinking about her son, and about what they had lived through together. None of it had to be lost with the arrival of a young woman, whom she could love, if only the woman would let her, but at the moment it all was gone completely, possibly forever. She noted with satisfaction that the rain did not invade the ground under the tarp.

When the rain had stopped, she left the camp, entered the forest and came to the chapel by the familiar path. It was the reason why she came here. Miraculous chapel, they said, granting prayers. For a while she looked at it in silence: a simple wooden structure with a steep roof over a miniature figurine of Virgin Mary surrounded by beads of different colours, ambers, artificial flowers and rosaries. What should she pray for? The words came slowly and then she knew and prayed.

***

The morning rose clear. She went to pray at the chapel and spent the rest of the day at the lake. She tried not let her thoughts go around in circles. What was. What could be. What is. She wanted to let the prayer work, as if it were medicine applied to alleviate pain.

In the evening, she set out again towards the lake. It was said that unusually bright Orion could be seen there and people gathered there to look at it. Some apparently recognized the brilliant reddish colour of the hunter's shoulder, the red supergiant Betelgeuse. How could that be possible, she thought, if the constellation could be seen from the Northern Hemisphere only in winter? Why would anyone want to see what was not there? But apparently, it was she, who was mistaken. She left the woods, took one of the roads, turned by the lodge, and suddenly stopped. Before her, windows lighted the front of the house. Behind one of them lay her host, an ex-pilot, now terminally ill. He was the same age as her father; during the war they were stationed a few kilometres from one another.

She stood there motionless, then sat on the bench from which his window was visible. She heard people at the lake, the cracking of the fire, the singing. She did not move for hours, did not lose the window from her sight.

***

That set a pattern for the next days. In the morning the prayer. She would turn from the road onto the rustling forest floor, stop before the slightly crooked chapel, look at the gentle face of Mary, and enter the space of prayer. As she prayed, something would move in the bushes, something would rattle, she would hear the jays' high pitched warnings. She never saw what it was. Maybe a deer or a wolf.

After the prayer, she would go to the beach with a blanket and a book. She would swim to a buoy and back. A wet bathing suit dried quickly in the sun.

In the evening she would sit on the bench in front of the house and look at the lighted window. The light must be coming from a bedside lamp. Maybe it stood at the sick man's bed. Something rose in her mind beyond the reach of formulated thoughts, and she waited patiently, letting it do so.

***

Suddenly, while sitting there, she wanted to listen to Mahler's Fourth Symphony. Long time ago, she put on the recording of it, when her son came home from school, and she was delighted to see how he listened attentively till the music was over. He never listened to any other classical piece of music with her. What did he like about this one? It is not an easy task to find Mahler's recording while camping, but she knew somebody in a cottage nearby, who kept a well-equipped music library. She was not disappointed.

The Fourth is believed to be the easiest of Mahler's symphonies, the shortest. Under the classic tones of the melodies of the first part there are dissonances, a dramatic, even tragic underscore. In the second movement, the violin solo appears—believed to be a personification of death—tuned a tone higher than it should be, unsettling and tense. And then, there is the fourth part, a child's song about Heaven, where the animals are slaughtered for the celestial feast.

When she listened to the music, a big black bear appeared on the road that passed through the forest. The neighbours called with the news in the middle of a song, the soprano voice mingling with the ringing of the phone.

***

The next day, a dense fog enveloped the lake and the surrounding woods. The water was glassy and bright beneath it. Life was lying in wait, looking at her as if something depended on her next move.

In a dream she had last night, she came to visit someone in a hospital but found the bed empty and already made. Pieces of clothing and shoes were left in disarray on the cover. Was it her father's bed? The pilot's? Or maybe her own? She did not want to think that it may have been her son's.

A movement in the fog caught her attention. She felt the urge to step on the lake, and to walk towards it, as if she could encounter there something even more surprising than walking on water.

She eased herself into the lake and swam. The water parted lazily, neither warm, nor cold. The sheen backed away, with encouragement rather than reluctance. She swam some more, then turned and swam back, feeling no regret about anything she could have missed. Out of the water, she looked back again. The brightness returned to the place where she first saw it, like a wild animal that does not let anyone approach, but does not escape either. She wondered if the chapel in the forest would become inaccessible because of the bear.

***

She dried herself and went to the lodge to call her son. The phone rang for a long time. What was she trying to achieve? The last time she called, she talked with her daughter-in-law, who later told her son that she was rude and unfriendly. She blushed remembering it. She was not able to treat anybody rudely, and was certain about the

friendliness of the conversation. But what if the young woman believed what she said? Was there something dark hidden deep inside
her, of which she was not even aware? They were so happy together,
the young woman and her son, clearly very much in love.

Only that counts, she had told her son, when they still talked.
Oh, how they used to talk!

I have to believe my wife, her son had said. She would have
agreed with him wholeheartedly if not for the implication of which
she suddenly became aware: I have to believe my wife so I have to
stop believing my mother.

She never questioned her daughter-in-law's behaviour with her
son again.

***

After the fog, the day became sunny and more beautiful than ever,
but in the late afternoon dense clouds came from the other side of
the lake, and a thunderstorm cracked overhead. She walked around
her camp in a raincoat and galoshes checking the ropes of the tarp,
lowering the masts so the rainwater would not gather in it. The
temperature dropped, but she stayed out, bumping up the tarp with
the back of her hand, from time to time. The water slushed out. In
between the spasms of lightning it became as dark as in the evening. What was the bear doing in such weather, she wondered, immediately scolding herself for sentimentality.

Suddenly, a lightning cracked, and a thunder followed. A pine
on the other side of the meadow burst into flames and she gasped,
transfixed, but the fire diminished almost immediately and disappeared.

***

In the next couple of days, the bear visited cottages, damaged some
garbage bins, tested garage doors. It was very big and not at all timid.

It charged towards people, when caught in the act. It was they who hid, looking through the windows into its malicious eyes, while it lingered about.

She went to see a damaged car nearby. The bear's claws pierced the back door. Inside, strawberries were forgotten for a night. The cottagers provided everybody with unsolicited advice: You happen upon the bear, make yourself look bigger, make noise. Back away really, really slowly, somebody said, and at least four people stopped him dead in his tracks: That's for a grizzly, this one is a black bear. She looked and listened, thinking: What if I call my son again? I may tell him about the bear. Eventually, she did not.

The district forest management was informed, and it promised to bring a cage for the bear. When people started to speak about not one, but two bears marauding, nobody called back to correct the information. There were indeed two of them; the sightings of the other one, smaller, maybe younger, following its bigger companion, were confirmed by cottagers.

***

She was invited for drinks on the beach. A table had been placed off the sand, between two small copses separating the beach from the meadow. Someone covered the table with a tablecloth, and bowls of fruits were put there, glasses full of alcoholized punch. The mood was one of celebration without a cause. She looked around, un-expectedly curious what these people do in the city, when vacations are over. Teachers? Doctors? Real estate agents? She recognized only their summer selves.

She pointed to the fruits: What about the bear?

What about it? asked someone in return. It's the middle of the day.

It was the middle of the day yesterday, when the bear trashed a garage door at some cottage, but she did not say it. Everybody knew. Maybe she was thinking about the bear more seriously than others. Or maybe she was more childish about it, as if trying to commune with the animal. Which possibly amounted to the same thing: only a child can give a proper significance and due respect to something like a bear.

***

Her son and his wife told her that a baby was coming. She imagined this little life as lying under the earth, ready to germinate like a sprout in spring. She shivered, when they talked about the baby too loudly, too openly. Better not. Better let her grow a little more. Her son accused her of not wanting the child, probably repeating what his wife said. She did not pay attention. Grow, she whispered to the fragile being, grow.

Her son's in-laws came to town, and she went to meet them for the first time since the wedding. They were loudly enthusiastic about the baby and cheering, and she watched them, amused. Couldn't, in fact, stop smiling, believing that her smile represented a solidarity with the kind of wild enthusiasm very foreign to her. Her joy was like a dawn—silent and enormous. Her passions were simply not a public affair.

Later, her son told her that she insulted everybody with her smile, with her arrogance. With believing that she was better. Did he hear it from his young wife? He had never been that critical of his mother.

She thought that it would pass, but it did not. She was told that she had not wanted her son married, that it had showed on her face during the wedding. How could anybody judge what occurred inside her with such certainty? She thought about her father. He had never talked about things like love but had she ever doubted it? Maybe better that he died before it all, she told herself, grabbing a blanket and a book on the way to the beach.

She spread the blanket on the warm sand, put the book down and suddenly stopped. How stiff she must have seemed to them, she thought. The realization surprised her. How cold she was, compared to their volcanic enthusiasm. She chuckled, shaking her head at the image.

***

But her son—he knew her better! Or he should have. At his birth she was overwhelmed with love that could have drowned her. The nurse took him away and she thought: I will never again be alone, which proved true but in a different way than she had expected. She thought it precisely at the moment of separation, even if only temporary.

Of course, she could have joined in the jubilation, making joyful noises and other visible signs of enthusiasm. Did her son expect her to do that, and did he feel disappointed when she did not? The problem was, she did not know how to do such things. She was certain that the falseness of it would be clearly visible. Others probably knew. Not that they pretended—she did not want to use that word—but rather adapted. Translated themselves into acceptable gestures and appropriate use of language. She preferred to find herself in a new situation, rather than to lose herself in it. She wanted nothing better than to accept her daughter-in-law easily, and in a matter-of-fact way. Even the thought about it raised in her the kind of joy that was curiously unfamiliar, and even more tempting because of that.

***

The cage finally arrived, and she went with a group of people to see it. A sort of a trailer supported a big pipe, closed with a solid grate at both ends. At one side the grate was lifted, held up to form a trapdoor. It was menacing. People came closer, so she did too. Something wriggled in the underbrush, and those present shivered nervously, but it was only a chipmunk, escaping into blueberries. She looked inside. There were crumbs of doughnuts as a bait. Chipmunks ran here and there, trying to carry it all out. It was clear that nobody would catch a bear here.

She was glad. She did not want the bear to be caught. At least not before she would get a chance to see it herself. Something, she thought, was to happen during that encounter. The bear blocked her access to the chapel and the possibility of prayer at the miraculous place. The bear, then, constituted a sign. A message. Maybe that her prayer was already answered.

***

She waited for the bear.

***

Finally, people reacted to the news about the bears, and the camping grounds slowly deserted. She, apart from not going to the chapel, lived exactly as before. Sitting on a bench at night and looking at the gentle light in the window, she thought about her son's new family. Faces. Gestures. Words. The intensity of her daughter-in-law's expectations tired her but, for the first time, she thought that maybe it was the deficiency of her own heart.

She was not scared at all. She knew what attracted bears. After the last meal she collected all the food in the cooler and brought it over to the lodge, making certain that fruits and sweets in particular were not forgotten. Washed thoroughly the dishes and the table upon her return. Looked over for any edible debris and only then turned off the lamp, went to the tent, fell asleep.

***

One evening, whoever was still there gathered on the porch of the lodge. Bottles of beer were passed around, when they heard a loud bang from the forest. Everybody thought the same: the bear got caught.

They wanted to go right away, take flashlights and go, but remembered that there were two bears, not one, and who knows, maybe the bear's companion loitered around the cage not knowing what to do next. Or maybe it was the younger bear that got caught, not experienced enough to know how to avoid pipes smelling of doughnuts and the other one, big and menacing, more and more angry, waited for people to shine their flashlights into its eyes.

For the first time she had trouble sleeping.

***

She woke suddenly. It was dawn. Her heart beat so fast as if she had just finished a run. She stepped out of the tent.

Maybe five meters from her stood an enormous black bear. It looked straight at her. Then, he wrinkled its nose, lifted its head and sniffed loudly. She felt its sharp reek.

She stood completely still, unafraid. Birds did not sing, trees did not rustle. There was in that silence an unfazed and overwhelming gentleness, no, more than that—love. She knew what it was with absolute certainty. The silence was coming inside her with every breath, and she also became more and more silent. Emptier. For a moment she felt as if she did not exist at all. And then she became new.

She did not know how long it lasted. The bear sniffed some more and walked away, shuffling its feet. A smaller bear burst out of the bushes, sent her one skittish look and also disappeared.

***

The same day, she packed up her camping gear, returned to the city and wrote a letter to her son and his wife: Dear children, she wrote, I am your mother and will never cease to be one. I do and will love you always. You may decide not to see me, but it will not change a thing.

POLISH WEDDING

Katherine Koller

AUNTIE MAGDA'S GETTING married.

Everyone is surprised and we can hardly wait to meet Lowell, her fiancé. She has kept him a secret, and has never even brought him over for Sunday dinner or anything, but says they've been seeing each other for a while.

Babcia is beyond delighted. She is in ecstasies. She even made *chruściki*. Auntie Magda will finally wear the dress lovingly created for her many years ago and, of course, it still fits. Babcia will bead it now. And then, she says, she may quit sewing. Her eyes are tired, even though they twinkle. Her eyes want a wedding.

Little birdie, don't wait so long like Ciocia Magda. She's hard on my heart.

I don't know why Auntie Magda is getting married at all, because she likes being on her own. But then I'm introduced to Lowell. He shakes my hand.

He met Auntie Magda at his orthodontics office. She wanted a little tooth straightening and found herself a fiancé! Babcia has always wanted a Polish doctor for her Magda, but with Lowell, the doctor part cancels out the need for the Polish part in her equation. For my Dad, who is neither Polish nor a doctor, Babcia invented a new formula that perfectly describes him: Handsome, Handy, with Height, and Holy.

Of Babcia's essential four Hs for husbands, Lowell's got the Handsome part totally covered, but he's not Handy at all. He says he's not outdoorsy. He lives in a condo and buys everything new. Auntie Magda laughs that he replaces anything that doesn't work the same day. I once saw him throw his cell phone against the wall. He may have his nails manicured, because they look polished. They are in better shape than mine. His skin is definitely moisturized. And tanned, but Auntie Magda tells me he fake bakes, at a tanning salon. It makes his teeth look whiter, for clients, she says. He's tall enough, but not enough Height to change a light bulb. Not his thing, anyway.

And he's not Holy. He laughed at that one. But Babcia doesn't seem to care. She is swept away, as are we all, by his looks: dark curly hair, straightest of bleached smiles, and a stubble beard that Auntie Magda often strokes with her fingers before he catches her hand and kisses it. I think I'm in love, too.

The wedding is going to be at the Holy Rosary Polish church, but there will be no mass. This, Babcia is willing to accept. At this point, with her pearl Magda permanently thirty-nine years old, Babcia keeps her mouth zipped.

But to me, she says, I whisper the mass, in Polish, and no one in the church knows, but it counts. My angels help me.

I am going to be the bridesmaid! Actually, junior bridesmaid because I'm only fifteen, but really because there is no groomsman. Lowell has a cousin but he can't make the trip, from Australia. Stella is eleven, too old to be a flower girl, but she is anyway, so it will only be us sisters walking up the aisle for our Auntie Magda.

No one wants Babcia to make Stella and me dresses, because she tires easily now and is having trouble seeing, but she says these are her last dresses, for her little birdie and little Sasha, which is what she still calls Stella, and she will do it. But I need to help. We pick the simplest of designs, an empire waist for both, and she has been saving the most exquisite satin, off-white, like the bridal gown, but with no beading or veil. Thank goodness.

I have to get all the way undressed for the fitting. Babcia slides the strong yet smooth palms of her hands around my bare middle. The tops of her hands are gnarly and papery.

Such a nice waist, she says. You keep it. Keep your waist.

She takes such care over my dress. I could wear it for my own wedding if, like Auntie Magda, I keep my waist. Babcia adds lace to the bodice, and it makes me feel like a bride-to-be, which I am, as a maid of honour. We cry a little when it is done. I tell her that I'll wear the dress at my own wedding, no matter what. She's already thought of that. She's made the side seams extra large in case I need to take it out a little, later, much later, for when I marry. If I ever do.

Make sure you marry. No be alone all your life. You make food anyway. So? Make enough for two. Why not with a man to make you feel like a queen?

I wonder if cooking for Lowell will make Auntie Magda feel like a queen, or if he'd ever throw the dish against the wall.

But Babcia is thinking of Dziadziu. And feels like a queen, even after all these years he's been gone. Her jewel eyes of spruce blue sparkle when she remembers him and her head lifts as if she was wearing a crown. I haven't noticed that shining yet in Auntie Magda's eyes, or Lowell's. In fact, I haven't seen them look into each other's eyes yet. Lowell often inspects his hands.

Auntie Magda takes Babcia and me to the cemetery to tell Dziadziu about her wedding even though Lowell had to cancel at the last minute, because he's had to rebook patients for today to take the week off for the honeymoon later. Babcia isn't too upset that Lowell and Dziadziu won't "meet." Mom thinks it's because Auntie Magda has been close to marrying several times, but always backed out, so again Babcia says nothing. Babcia wears a gorgeous fuchsia silk kerchief tied up tight even though it's a warm fall day and Auntie Magda keeps the top of her convertible up. Because Mom and Stella can't come either, I am the only one from our branch of the family to go to the cemetery.

It's going to be a small family wedding. We only have three weeks to prepare, so I am over at Babcia's for a few weekends working on my dress and Stella's. Babcia lets me tack down the facings and do the pressing. Auntie Magda wants the wedding before the winter, so Babcia doesn't have to go out in the cold. Since her pacemaker,

Babcia moves slower. She constantly rests her hand on her heart, as if the pacemaker is a pet, or another hand.

The doctor said Babcia should eventually forget that it's there. But I don't, she says.

She talks to it. She scolds, Too fast, like a toy clown, you wind me up!

Sometimes, abruptly, she has to sit down. We've brought a folding chair, so she won't kneel for her prayers by the graveside, but she does anyway, using the chair only to get down and up. My job is to take the old flowers and put them in a plastic bag. Babcia likes to crumble and sprinkle the dried up Dziadziu flowers over her vegetable garden to keep away slugs. Next I have to wipe out the metal vase with some paper towel. Then I pour water from a 7-Up bottle into it while Babcia adds her blessings to the already holy water.

I also get to unwrap and arrange the new flowers, brought by Auntie Magda from the florist: brilliant irises, the rich blue of the autumn sky; yellow chrysanthemums, Babcia's favourite; and red gerbera daisies with straws around their stems to support their heavy heads. I add the greens last, cedar boughs. I smell them first, so fresh and woodsy. I know the green will far outlast the blue, yellow and red. The flowers look even more intense against the black gravestone, black like the coal my Dziadziu mined in the river valley, far below the roots of any trees where he made rooms in the rock from the very coal he shovelled and, car by car, sent outside to the sun. When the boys and I found his miner's headlamp in the jumbled garage, an island in her garden, Babcia let me keep it to remind me of him. I wish it still worked, for night sketching. Charlie and Tom found pieces of coal to keep, and even played street hockey at Babcia's with a flat puck piece.

In the cemetery corner stand tall Norway spruce. Their branches try to reach up but droop down like curtains. Some entwined, holding each other's crossing branches. They must have been planted a hundred years ago to protect their ground people from wind and noise. When I walk near enough to touch them, I feel the heat of the afternoon sun radiating from their boughs. Charlie and Tom and Stella and I used to play in them, shooed off to expend our energy away from where Babcia knelt, on Easter visits to Dziadziu.

Today Babcia is not sad. She has that glow, like a queen. She and Auntie Magda are speaking Polish. I didn't know that Auntie Magda still could, and then I recognize the prayer. I think it's the "Our Father" because I hear the word for bread, *chleba,* as in "Give us this day, our daily bread." I wonder if bread really means bread here, or time, "our day." I realize that my time, my day, is not the same as Babcia's and it helps me be patient for these prayers to end. So we can have tree cake, *sękacz,* a sponge cake with a cross-section of dark and light layers, like the growth rings in the trunk of a tree. But it's *boughten,* in a little Bon Ton Bakery box tied with string, so Babcia hardly has any and declines to leave some for Dziadziu as she usually does when it's her own. It's definitely not the same, much sweeter, but I happily eat the rest of hers and Auntie Magda's after her usual one bite only.

Auntie Magda says, Just like Charlie and Tom!

No, I say, they'd be fighting over it.

Cassie's still growing, says Auntie Magda.

So we hem your dress last thing, says Babcia.

Auntie Magda lights a thick white candle with a deep well for the wick, which protects the flame from the soft breeze when we leave. She resists lighting a cigarette during the entire outing, because of Babcia, who has trouble breathing. Although I suspect coal dust, Babcia blames Dziadziu's death on his heavy smoking.

So Auntie Magda chews Nicorette gum when she's with Babcia, snapping it. It's usually Mom who brings Babcia for her Dziadziu visit because Auntie Magda is always working. She has never liked cemeteries. You can tell by the colours she wears: today she is in the hottest of pinks. But she prays to her dead father, here with her mother, that her marriage will be loving and long. At least I think that's what she's saying. I don't understand the language, but I am the sole witness. Me, and the trees.

At the wedding, in my two-inch cream heels, I walk tall like Auntie Magda made me practice. Dad agreed to escort her up the aisle, but not give her away, because as he says, Auntie Magda is her own person, not a dame to get or give. Mom is in the front row, and supports Babcia's arm when she stands up. Babcia is smiling, and Mom smiles at me, too, but she still seems less thrilled than the rest of us.

But Auntie Magda is bringing us an Uncle Lowell, I want to whisper to Mom. Maybe it's the rush we've been in to get ready. She's had a lot to do, like getting the boys in suits. When did they get so good looking? Charlie and Tom both have Dziadziu's dark hair and a day-old beard. They each have a dolled-up blonde girlfriend on their arm. But I feel like a princess, like Babcia says I am, and she gives a little clap when I pass her, holding the flowers, creamy roses. If Auntie Magda is the queen today, Babcia is the queen mother! She's always adored her.

During the ceremony, Babcia speed-recites the entire Mass in Polish, like she said she would. After, I put on my creamy fleece cape that Babcia made last night, in case it is cold on my arms, and it is, for October 31st. (Halloween was the only available date at the church.) I step elegantly, holding up my swishy gown, into the limousine with Auntie Magda and Uncle Lowell. I want to be the first one to call him that.

They light up cigarettes like they've been waiting all day, and drink from a silver flask they've stashed in the limo. It's engraved with their initials: L and M. They offer me some, and I want to, but I suddenly feel like the kid niece and I don't want to take the chance of dripping on my dress. I tell them about Babcia's private silent Mass. Auntie Magda laughs. Uncle Lowell checks his phone.

I ask Uncle Lowell if I get to dance with him.

If you want, he says.

Auntie Magda nudges him.

Sure, he says. You pick the dance.

I have my hair done in an up-do. It's got too much stinky hairspray, but it holds in the wind for pictures. We shiver for plenty of those, with multiple photographers, in the trees by the Legislature after the wedding. By the time we get to the reception, I'm starving.

The beautiful wedding dinner is at the Macdonald Hotel. The decorations are exquisite, all live greens and creams. We have a few speeches, even a short one from Babcia, who gets teary and tongue-tied, ending up in Polish that only Auntie Magda and Mom understand, because they cry, too. Later Mom tells me what she said: *Dziękuję Bogu za rodzinę, przyjaciół i dziedzictwo*, thank God for family, friends and my heritage. People have stopped listening and I get up and escort Babcia back. It's bad for her heart to get upset. She kisses me after we're seated again at the head table, and some of her tears wet my cheek. I leave them there because they are tears of joy.

She says to me, *Kocham cię.*

I love you too, Babcia.

Now, there is no one for her to worry about. Unless, now it's me.

I wait for my chance with Uncle Lowell, but he never catches my eye because he's busy dancing with Auntie Magda. They look so good together in the golden light that everyone else only watches them. Charlie and Tom's bleached blonde girlfriends in their little boutique dresses and borrowed pearls are also in awe, but they were sure chatting each other up while Babcia gave her speech. Then, even Charlie and Tom looked at each other in solidarity, but they didn't say anything to the girls.

After the speech, I'm in a washroom stall and I overhear the blonde girlfriends.

So boring!

I was dying!

How can they stand it?

I come out with my best two-inch heel posture and say, Because she's Babcia.

The girls blink at me. But I'm not finished.

You know how Charlie and Tom say the Eagle has landed? From

when the guy walks on the moon? That's what this wedding means to her. Not cool.

They dash out of the washroom. They don't even say sorry. I hope I never see them again.

Later I nibble on wedding cake, and realize that the bride and groom have also vanished, to change. They return in their going-away outfits. They are off to Hawaii for their honeymoon, both in stylish cream cruise wear that matches the roses in the room. Everyone takes photos. The band plays for them, and Dad brings Babcia back halfway through the song because she's had enough, her hand on her heart, and he takes me to the dance floor. In my heels, I'm almost his height. Dad's eyes smile and wrinkle at me. I used to stand barefoot on his shoes when we danced. This turns out to be the last dance. The band packs up, we gather up the gorgeous flowers to take home and my night as maid of honour is over.

Not long after that, the many phone calls from Auntie Magda to Mom suggest that the marriage is done, too. Mom quilts, her head at an angle to support the phone. Mom's needle rides through layers of fabric in silent logical lines, while Auntie Magda's wails unravel her fantasy tapestry. No one says anything to Babcia.

THE LAST REFUGE

Lilian Nattel

ANYONE WHO HAD nowhere else to go could camp out on Uncle Frank's porch as long as they didn't expect him to talk. He lived where the Great Lakes lowland gives way to the oldest stone on earth, having eroded over the course of a billion years from lofty mountains to a shield of pink granite. His house was made of wooden planks. It consisted of the porch, a back room with a bed, and a front room warmed by a wood stove. His fridge was a recent acquisition. To avoid going to the hospital, he'd illegally hooked up his house to the grid, using the fridge, which he'd found at the dump, to keep his medication from spoiling. He had a canoe under the porch and a clear path to the lake. When I was sixteen, right after I got my driver's licence, I came on a sunny day in early summer to take him out on the water.

"Do you want to see your kids?" I asked. I was paddling the canoe from the shallows where lilies grow to the cold deeps surrounded by rocky cliffs. He still smoked though he was near to leaving this earth, and he offered me an unfiltered cigarette. I shook my head.

"I want a lot of things." Uncle Frank drew a deep drag on his cigarette, holding it between his thumb and index finger. "I am a mean old bugger."

Dipping the paddle in the water, I turned the canoe away from the rocks and paddled carefully with long even strokes, trying not to jar my uncle. "You're all right."

"Compared to your father maybe." Uncle Frank laughed and coughed. "Compared to a human being, I'm a mean son of a bitch."

Uncle Frank and my father grew up in a rundown suburb of Windsor. Grandpa was a wagon maker who bought the first car dealership in Ford City and made a fortune driving liquor across the border to Detroit during Prohibition. He could have moved anywhere, but he stayed in Ford City because my grandmother hated it: dingy, chaotic, smelling of Polish sausage. He never hit her. However, he was known to bundle up the entire dinner as unfit for pigs, put it in the trash, and go out to eat by himself. Grandma bore everything quietly until she was diagnosed with cancer at the age of thirty-seven. With the same quietude, she refused treatment and left the only way she could. After she died, Frank ran away. But my dad stayed, went to university, became a lawyer and married a woman, not a mouse. My father had a long list of rules, which he changed as he pleased. My mother was adept at accommodation. She had grown up under German occupation and knew how to operate in a totalitarian regime. But I never knew when my father was going to turn on me.

I was nine the first summer I was sent to Uncle Frank's as punishment. There was no electricity and no running water on his property. I had to pump water, milk the cow, slop the pigs and shuck corn by hand. I was meant to leave at the end of summer with calluses and an appreciation of the comforts of home. But Uncle Frank had only two rules: don't rest till you're done, and keep the animals clean. He himself was none too clean, nor too fragrant.

"She was right to take off with the kids," he said. He seldom talked about his ex-wife and never by name. I was kneeling in the stern, Uncle Frank in the bow with his back to me. "Don't even know where they are. And I'm not going to try to find them so they can come back and feel sorry for a stranger."

Motor boats weren't allowed in this part of the lake. It was as quiet as it had been centuries ago when an artist had stood up in a canoe to draw with red ochre on the great rocks. The canoe shifted gently as water lapped at its side. A heron was perched on an outcropping, so close that I could see the feathers on its long neck, ruffled by the breeze. My brother and sister joked about Uncle Frank's place. They didn't know a thing about it.

"I always had a good time here," I said.

"Was it the gourmet meals?" He looked as sick as he was, but he'd never looked good, drinking more than he ate, smoking more than either. Corn didn't grow on his land anymore. There was nobody left to work it. He flicked the cigarette away. He lit another. "Or when I beat your hide?"

"You never laughed at me." My father liked a good joke. My brother had to sleep in the cobwebby basement because he was afraid of spiders. Dad made me eat a raw steak to cure me of being a vegetarian. If I swallowed every bite, I wouldn't have to strip down. But it wasn't the violation that made me wake up in a sweat. It was the mocking pleasure in his face.

The first night I was at Uncle Frank's, he got drunk and walloped me with the double issue of *Hunting Digest*. When he passed out, I stood there, looking down at his prone body. Then I went out to look for a branch that had a good swish, and with it, I returned the favour. It's fortunate that I wasn't bigger or I might have done serious damage. If that had been my father, as, in some inchoate part of my reptilian brain I was imagining, when he woke up, I'd have been raw steak on a plate. If I could have skipped over the chewing and gotten right to the bare dead bone, I'd have gone for it. But I wanted to avoid the painful interim, and so I hid out in the woods in back of the house for two days. The third day I was so thirsty, I crept back, hoping to get a drink from the water barrel unseen.

Uncle Frank was sitting on the porch. He had a gun. He said that I ought to learn to shoot because if you want to kill someone, beating them up just means they will come back for you.

I said: *Are you coming back for me?* And Uncle Frank said: *Not this time. Looks like you have a mind of your own, and if so, you are the exception to my brother's family. If you work hard, I might let you return to this paradise.* I said: *I just need to get some water.*

He moved, and I jumped back, but Uncle Frank said that he wouldn't drink while we worked the farm. We shook on it. And he kept his word. Six days a week he was sober. On Sundays he drank, and I hid out in the woods, taking food and water and a poncho in case it rained. He smacked me one from time to time because I did something careless or dangerous, left ripe corn on the stalk or mishandled an axe. He taught me to swim in the lake. I stayed up until the sky was a bowl of stars, and Uncle Frank taught me their names. I learned that nights could be safe. A man could be fair. At the end of the summer, he shook my hand and said he liked me enough, and I could come back if I felt like it. When I was home and humiliated, I thought of the farm. *You're the exception,* I'd say to myself, and half-believed it was a good thing.

There would be serious payment for sneaking away in Mom's car. My thighs tensed when I thought of it. But Uncle Frank wasn't going to last until I got out of that house. I'd come to say goodbye and to take something with me to remember him by. A stone from the side of the lake or, more appropriately, I thought in my cynical moments, a rusty nail. We were silent for a long time, Uncle Frank smoking and coughing while I paddled away from the faded paintings of horned creatures, animal and human, the sun warm on my face as I made my way to the other end of the lake.

There, where water lilies were pink and white, cottages had been built, torn down, and built up bigger. The weekends were noisy with drinkers speeding in their boats. Developers were after Uncle Frank's land, but they would have to wait until he had finished dying. The way in was overgrown with bush. I had parked Mom's car at the edge of the property and hiked in for a half hour. The last developer who had tried that had hiked out again at high speed, having been met by a couple of mangy dogs selected for the unappealing look of their fur and the vitality of their teeth.

In the night Uncle Frank was cold, so I lay next to him, keeping the bed warm with the warmth of my own body, which my uncle had hit but never invaded. We lay side by side, touching at the shoulders. All through the night, Uncle Frank spoke of the stars and their sad stories. Outside, the dogs barked from time to time. After he ran out of stories, he watched the crescent moon rising. "Even a shit like me doesn't want to die," he said. "Not with my life being a complete waste."

"It wasn't," I said. "Not to me. So shut up about it."

When morning came, my uncle took his shot and we had raw hotdogs for breakfast, there being no wood for the wood stove. Before hiking out to the car, I said goodbye, giving him my hand to shake. Uncle Frank took it between his. Then he put his arms around me for the first time, the last time, this imperfect man, my uncle, the drunk, the one person who had stood between me and despair. He hugged firmly, strongly, passing along the last of himself, giving me all that remained of the goodness he had hidden and hoarded and doled out with miserly reluctance, because love is not restricted to those worthy of offering it, so that in the end he had this to give, this memory, this memento, this pilot light that burned in the cold and the dark.

BUT HER FACE

Lisa McLean

WHEN ELA WAS younger, she wore her hair in thick ponytails that draped over her shoulders like an elegant scarf. A jeweller friend of her mother's once likened her particular shade of strawberry blond to pink gold. For Ela, the description itself was enough to treasure.

She tried not to be vain because she knew it was an unattractive trait. But she tucked compliments like that one away and brought them out again when she felt most anxious. At nineteen, she was mortified to admit that, as the surgeon began to speak, she was returning to thoughts about her beautiful hair.

Words like *benign* and *malignant* had no place in the conversation yet, the doctor said. There was a tumour. It would be removed, but it would be tricky. One step at a time, he said, he would do everything he could.

She nodded her head up and down and felt the heavy pull of her hair, hanging flat, still damp from that morning's shower. She imagined herself bald, her body full-to-bursting from drug side effects, as her grandmother had been before she died.

Ela resisted the urge to search *neck tumour* on her phone. She rubbed her index finger over the mound that had become her talisman, with her for half a year. It grew from the ticklish spot on her neck, at the base of her ear. It seemed more of a curiosity than a hindrance. She'd had cysts before, and they had always dissolved as her family doctor said they would. So when she felt the lump on her neck grow more persistent, instead of making a special trip home from school to see a doctor, she gave her cyst a name: Fiona.

Ela started saying things like "Fiona and I are staying in to study tonight" or "Fiona needs a shower." It was all in fun—an eccentric way to make the best of an oddity. It never occurred to her that Fiona could be something more sinister. She confessed all of this to her mother over frozen yogurt. The two of them picked at their paper cups of soft serve that had turned to puddles among mounds of candy bar.

"This isn't how I thought my first semester of university would go," she said.

Eventually her mother scraped her chair across the floor and they both stood. Her mother's warm hands reached out and pressed against the lump, working her fingers around it to test its boundaries. Ela watched the reflection of their awkward embrace in the darkening glass of the restaurant window. She saw her posture had defaulted to her boxing stance.

***

She had been boxing for a few months by then, just enough to learn the basics. She signed up for a trial month with some girls from her floor, but Ela was the only one of them to return on the second week. There was something in the way Damon showed her how to stand —how he kicked lightly at her feet until they fell into place, how he instructed her to angle her body—that made her see she'd been doing everything wrong. When she was in position he stood behind her and pulled on her shoulders to judge how she kept her balance.

The gym was an old garage with a grubby cement floor and a regulation-sized boxing ring in the corner. Along one wall, meat hooks dangled heavy bags from the broken ceiling tiles. A child's tricycle and an empty rain barrel were inexplicably stored in the corner beside the stereo. Before each class she wrapped her hands more or less the way Damon had shown her, while assuming her boxing stance.

"Good," Damon had said. "You're a natural fighter."

***

Back at school after meeting the surgeon, Ela's affection for Fiona had waned. She told her friend Kate: "Fiona and I are breaking up. Let's go out." They blew off their night class and Ela spent an hour styling her hair until it fell in soft, textured layers around her shoulders.

At the bar, they got drunk on two-dollar shooters that were so sweet they made their teeth ache. Kate kept telling Ela in gushy drunk-girl tones that whatever Ela needed, she would be there.

"My aunt had breast cancer last year," Kate said, cupping her own breasts to communicate over the noise. The drinks were slowing Ela down, dulling her anxiety the way she'd hoped. She twirled her hair off her neck to cool off and accidentally grazed Fiona with the back of her hand.

"We had a boob party, the night before my aunt's surgery," Kate said. "Everyone wore sexy bras with no shirts. We had boob cups my mom found online. We even had a boob cake—a life-sized bust." Kate was gesticulating now. Measuring her own torso, and using her hands to show the approximate size of the cake.

"The worst part?" Kate was saying. "We hadn't thought the cake thing through. When it was time for dessert, no one wanted to cut into it. It was too much of a visual."

Ela felt the weight of the drinks in her gut. She slid her bum across the bench seat toward the tall guy at the end, and observed his friends instinctively stepping away to give them space. He leaned his head into Ela's, his ear against her mouth. She breathed the smell of spices—paprika and something else.

"Fiona would like a beer now," she said. She was trying on a foreign version of herself. She cocked her head. Licked her lips.

"Chris was hoping you'd say that, Fiona," he said.

***

Ela arrived at her mother's house the night before her surgery with a bag full of laundry and her books. It could have been any other weekend visit from school. Her mother *tsk-tsked* at the damage boxing had done to her hands, at the way crisp strokes of fresh blood outlined her knuckles.

"Aren't you supposed to wear gloves at the gym?" she said. "What about hand wraps?" As if it had never occurred to Ela to find out what equipment might be required for boxing.

They watched their favourite show and ate schnitzel sandwiches in front of the television. At eleven her mother brought out a tray of *krówki* and gingerbread. Tall glasses of Orangeade.

"Last call," she said. There would be nothing to eat or drink after midnight. When they'd had their fill, Ela fell asleep with her head on her mother's lap. Fiona was a firmness between them.

***

The worst hangover Ela ever had was after that night out with Kate. She spent most of the morning-after on the tiled bathroom floor of her residence, her floor mates keeping one toilet stall open for when she needed to throw up. Ela remembered thinking, this is what chemo will be like, only without the hair, and the people.

She meant to go home with Chris that night. To have a one-night stand and knock it off the list of student experiences she thought she should have before it was too late.

"Your friend is funny," Chris had said to Ela. They leaned against a tall table, cardboard coasters gone soft and wet under their cold bottles.

Kate was already sitting on Chris' roommate's lap. She was pointing at her chest and Ela hoped she wasn't telling the story about the boob party again.

"We've only known each other for a few months," Ela slurred. Something in her speech made her think of her grandmother's accent, the shortness of it, the way it crowded the tongue. "She's alright for a butterface." It was a term remembered from high school. *Nice body, but 'er face ...* Ela had never used it in a sentence, and hearing herself say it about a friend caught her by surprise. Made her sick. Made her certain that Fiona was gaining a stronger foot-hold. She swished the beer in her mouth and savoured the bitter taste of hops.

There was something in the way Chris looked at Ela—the slow blink searching for focus that made her see he was drunker than he let on. The slowness of it made her think of an iguana. There was something ugly and cold-blooded about them both.

She wanted to punch Chris. She imagined slipping her right shoulder and using the momentum of her hips to hit him hard in the side of the gut with a left uppercut. She would dip low again and come back with a right.

Instead she heard the shrill mean-girl cackle that had erupted from deep within her core. The laughter was so powerful it made her eyes drip, and left them both gasping for breath. *Butterface*, she breathed. It was the queerest thing she'd said in ages. It was a relief to be so unlike herself.

"You're a cool chick, Fiona," Chris said then. He clinked his beer bottle with hers. She didn't bother to correct him.

***

In those first few days after her surgery, rootless in the waves of pain medication, Ela dreamed about boxing. She reviewed every les-son she had. Imagined herself leaner and stronger than ever. Da-mon was calling out combinations and she threw them as they came. When she woke, as the medication was wearing off, there was hurt. It was the throbbing in her neck where Fiona used to be, but there was tightness in her shoulders, her hips, her arms too.

Can you show me an *O*, the doctor asked. An *EEE?* His own mouth stretched exaggerated motions that Ela seemed unable to mimic. She caught the metallic glint of fillings in his back molars.

When Ela was ready to hear the answer she made a sound in her throat that brought her mother to her bedside. Her mother smiled too wide. Waited for Ela to return it.

"Tell me," Ela said.

"You did great," she said. "It's gone to biopsy."

Ela relaxed into the pillow. Cringed at the sting of bandages rubbing against her raw neck. She sucked on the side of a cheek that felt frozen from a trip to the dentist. Waited for her mother to speak again.

"*Kochanie,*" her mother said. "Fiona turned out to be a real bitch."

***

The week after her surgery, the doctor confirmed there had been no cancer. Ela carried with her a hand-drawn diagram of the finger-shaped muscles that extend from the neck. Her surgeon drew it as he spoke, had explained nerves were finicky. That there was always a chance, during surgery, that they—here he drew black *Xs*—that they would stop working, possibly permanently. He shaded areas where Fiona had knotted herself around the facial nerve. They were just pen-drawn shapes on the back of a prescription pad. They could have been anything. To Ela, they were everything.

Her right eye sagged downward and her mouth twigged up now. The word *grimace* came to her more than once. She joked, on her better days, that she had become an over-exaggerated caricature of herself. But laughing about it ended in feeling the awkwardness of her smile. The coolness of too much air on her teeth. Her eye was a merciless slow drip delivering a tear every few minutes. She swiped at it madly with the back of her hand.

To Kate, she said: "I really was ready to lose my hair if it came to it. People recognize a scarf around the head for what it is. But this?" She slapped lightly at the numb side of her face. "There's no easy way to explain this."

***

Ela spent Christmas break on her mother's couch watching the *Rocky* boxed set. She rubbed at her scar, which had the itch of healing.

Pieces of black stitches came away in her hand. When the itch got stronger she boarded a bus, resting the numb side of her face against the cool window.

The handful of guys at the gym hardly noticed when she set her bag on the bench and searched out her shoes. They were talking about a fighter in the Ultimate Fighting Championship. They were doing that dramatic cringe thing boys do when they lean forward and groan, mimicking the pain from a hit to the groin.

Damon turned the screen of his laptop so they could all see the clip. One fighter's leg curled all the way around another's, and Ela felt her stomach lurch when she realized the bone inside the skin snapped. It was a ribbon of saltwater taffy. Or a rolled hand wrap, unfurling. The moment was surprisingly poetic for something as gruesome as a compound fracture.

Ela was wrapping her hands when Damon appeared quietly beside her. "Haven't seen you for a while," he said. And then: "Jesus, you okay?"

Ela nodded. She found her place on the cement floor a little apart from the guys and she started to skip. The rhythmic nothingness of feet jumping over rope allowed her to turn off part of her brain that made her think of Fiona. She felt her shoulders relax and her breathing pick up as her body warmed to the activity. And when Damon warned them that there was only 30 seconds left to the round, it was the opposite of a snooze button. She picked up her pace and took the opportunity to make the most of the time. To work harder and faster than before.

When the buzzer signalled the end of the round, Damon bounded to the front of the room. He called out combinations of the numbers she had come to associate with motions, jabs and hooks. *One-two. One-two-three. One-three-three.* He told them to give it a try and then he paced the room, stopping to inspect and correct.

When he got to Ela, he shook his head. "I want you to move in front of the mirror," he said. "You have to look at your face. Your hands. Understand what goes where. Understand why."

Ela nodded. She tried to focus on the movement. Tried to act like watching her reflection was no big deal. When she tilted her head she saw the flash of the dark pink keloid path that began and ended on her neck. She let her hair down from its ponytail and shook her head until it blanketed that portion of the damage.

"Focus on the movement," Damon said. "Drill it until you get it."

She had been away for a month, but her body remembered. Ela positioned her body into her fighting stance once more and held her fists on the outside of her jawline the way Damon had shown her. She relaxed into the familiar pull of her muscles. She focused on the nuances of movement. It was the subtleties that mattered most. She narrowed her gaze, and dared herself to look, really look, at how each movement led to the next.

THE TOWER OF FOOLS

Małgorzata Nowaczyk

BENTLEY WATCHED ADÈLE pass without a glance at the hydrocephalic
skeleton of a five-year-old child hung on a yard-tall metal pole,
alien-headed, lights glaring on its glass case. She entered the next
room down the corridor that curved to his right. *Der Narrenturm,
The Tower of Fools.* Not very PC back in the 17th century, were they,
Bentley thought. The Museum of Anatomy and Pathology in the
old psychiatric ward of the Vienna General Hospital was housed in
a round, four-story tower separated from the main building by an
expanse of lawn. The physical specimens of contagion and birth
defects in two-hundred-year-old glass jars filled with murky fluid
only compounded the barbarity of the place. Bentley had to admit
that as far as medical horrors go it was a fitting setting. Thick,
whitewashed brick walls separated tiny cages of rooms on the outer
wall; a circular corridor surrounded an inner courtyard where he
imagined the less affected inmates had been allowed to take air. He
had expected the place to reek of formaldehyde, like the pathology
departments in all the hospitals where he had worked, but the
building was odourless, sterile.

He didn't want to come, not at all, but from the moment she
learned about it Adèle became obsessed. Once here, she went from
room to room, her eyes drawn from one specimen-containing jar to
another. She never did anything half-way. Studying, work, sex. Having a baby. In the Contagion Room Bentley was reminded of the
story Adèle told about the Plasticine models of a syphilitic she saw
as a child at a French venereology clinic. The new nanny her mother

had hired made Adèle promise not to tell anybody as she pulled her into the dark hallway and up the steep, wooden staircase. When the woman disappeared into the examining room, Adèle—curious, and a precocious reader—went from display case to display case, and made out the words letter by awful letter. *Gumma, congenital syphilis, primary chancre.* She was six years old. She had not been able to sleep for months afterwards, the speckled foetus and the caved-in nose floated in front of her every time she closed her eyes. Fifteen years later, during a medical school lecture on sexually transmitted diseases, she darted out from the lecture hall, her chair clanging to the floor. Bentley found her in the quadrangle, sucking on a cigarette. "I've seen those before." She choked back her tears before the story tumbled all out.

But today she marched past them. Two rooms later she stood, transfixed, and stared at a preserved baby with its intestines floating outside its abdomen, its little fingers interlaced as if in prayer, put in that position by some well-meaning—or was it morbid?—mortician, and slumped forward, its nose flattened against the glass of the jar. The look on Adèle's face must have been the look the child Adèle had in the venereology clinic—mouth slack, eyes darting about the specimen, taking in all the gruesome details. An anencephalic newborn in a jar behind her stared at Bentley from beneath half-closed eyelids.

He knew that he wouldn't be able to sleep that night.

***

A few days after she ran out of the lecture hall Adèle dragged Bentley into Fairweather's at Yonge and Eglinton. A rack in a back corner held a clutch of cocktail dresses, their cheap-looking fabrics glimmered in the bright ceiling lights.

"Ooh, can you imagine anything worse?" Adèle asked.

Bentley eyed the dresses.

"I *gotta* try them on!" Lemon yellow, violent pink, green, and neon mauve tumbled off the rack into her arms and she disappeared into the fitting room.

"Stupid cheap zipper." The words floated over the partition. "How's this?" Adèle flung the curtain aside and twirled out in the green dress. It cinched her around the waist, the straps drug into her shoulders; even though she was slim and toned she looked like a boiled ham in a netting. On a bed of stewed Boston lettuce. And yet, she was still beautiful.

Bentley pumped his index finger in his open mouth and made gagging sounds. He reached for the zipper. She weaseled out of his arms and ducked back behind the curtain. Soon she popped out in the neon blue.

"This colour does nothing for you."

"The colour? What about the cut? Those flounces! Whoever came up with this deserves to die a long-drawn out death in the seventeenth circle of hell. Drowned in tears of women who had to wear this horror."

"There were only nine circles of ..." he began to say, and Adèle rolled her eyes.

"I *know* that," she said.

The next dress, the mauve, made her pale, freckled skin look like *she* had secondary syphilis. He bit his lip as he remembered Adèle's shaking voice.

When she disappeared into the fitting room for the fourth time, he was ready to walk out and never come back.

"Did you have to try *all* of them?" he asked long after they left the store. Something in his voice made her stop and look at him.

"I thought it was funny," she said.

"You have no sense of proportion." He stomped off, leaving her standing alone at the entrance to the subway.

The following morning, he waited for her at the same spot. She was late. He had studied way past his bedtime to make up the time, and was feeling grouchy and unkind. But he couldn't go a morning without seeing her. He waved when he saw her in the crowd.

"Ready for the gynie exam?" Adèle asked when she reached him.

Bentley looked up at the trees just coming out in leaves. Greenish mist hung around the branches. No apologies from Adèle, ever. A sparrow trilled and went silent over their heads.

"I'm totally not," Adèle said. "This fertility crap. I have to put up with it every month, I don't want to study it, too."

"I thought procreation was every woman's passion," Bentley said carelessly. Adèle's cheeks went brick red.

"I'll have you know that I am not constantly thinking about babies and nursing and lactating and gestating and bringing life into this world and whatever other cliché crap you chauvinist misogynes think women are about."

"Sex?" Bentley asked just as Adèle inhaled to continue. He wiggled his black eyebrows like a beetle. Adèle snorted and punched him in the shoulder.

"Hah! I *am* like a guy in that respect, eh? Men think about sex ..."

"... every eight seconds," Bentley said, finishing with her.

Adèle laughed and leaned into him, her head on his shoulder. His penis stirred and thickened—obviously he was one of those men.

"You must have gotten too much testosterone exposure during your foetal life," he said. He kept his arm around her shoulder the rest of the way to the hospital.

The first time he saw Adèle she was dancing on a chair at their med school orientation party. She wore autographed boxer shorts from an upper class man, the prize token for the scavenger hunt; a wide grin—all teeth—split her face, thick brown hair parted in a bob on the right. As she shook it off her eyes met Bentley's and she winked at him, her face an invitation. Bentley felt his face grow hot.

They were sleeping together a month later. Bentley, virginal, realized right away that Adèle was much more experienced than he would allow himself to imagine. Her lipstick on his penis—kissing it, biting it, sucking it she smeared the crimson on the pearly pink of his shaft and foreskin. He pushed aside thoughts of the unnamed men, their greedy hands, their probing tongues and dicks that knew Adèle better than he did.

He realized then that he would never let go of her.

**

What are we doing here, Bentley wondered as he followed Adèle into another low-ceilinged room. And another. She had to see every last atrocity, every last crime nature committed against itself in forming these monsters. Teratogenesis—the study of monsters—he remembered from their genetics lectures. She shouldn't even be here. After all those miscarriages what could be going through her mind, for god's sake? What was she thinking as she stared at the specimens? Better no baby than one of those? All that blood she had lost with the last miscarriage, she almost needed a hysterectomy. It took her months to recover but she wouldn't allow a transfusion. She was still hoping she'd get pregnant after five years of tests and fertility treatments.

He loved her so much.

That night, after he rolled off her, Bentley lay supine on the king-size hotel bed, arms splayed. The neon sign from the cafe across the street flickered blue shadows across the curtains.

"I want to try IVF." Adèle rubbed her face in his hairy chest, a greying patch extending from nipple to nipple. "This ... this isn't working."

"This?"

"I'm not getting any younger." She had turned thirty-six in January.

"I'm not good enough?"

Adèle lifted her head and stared at him, unblinking.

"That's what you're saying, isn't it?" Bentley always lowered his voice as his temper rose.

"*I* had all those miscarriages." Her voice sounded wet. "We still don't know why I can't carry a baby to term."

She rose from the bed and stood by the window, her body dark against the sheer curtain. Outlined in blue, the curve of her hips and butt, broad as if made for bearing children, made him want her all over again. He grabbed her waist and pushed her face down onto the bed.

"I'll show you," he hissed through his teeth as he lowered his face beside hers. Adèle turned her head and Bentley saw her perfect profile. A tear streaked down across her cheekbone. He kissed it, tasted salt. His body sagged.

"I'm sorry," he whispered.

Adèle squirmed beneath him, turned over, and wrapped her arms around him, scissored her legs across his buttocks.

"Don't ever leave me," she said.

***

The next morning Bentley woke up with an erection. Something tugged at his consciousness. A nagging, unpleasant something. Adèle, in a backless, shimmering silver-grey gown, the even beads of her spine bisecting her back with such grace it took his breath away. She turned and his penis flatlined. Bentley shook his head to dislodge the image: a line of blood down Adèle's belly, from the ribcage to the pubic bone, in a perfect parallel to her spine, the dress gaping open, muscle and fascia slashed, a glistening globe of the uterus exposed. The bottom half of a baby hung out from the incision, buttocks and legs hanging. Pulsating coils of umbilical cord dangled down to Adèle's knees, blood stains splashed down to the hem of the gown.

The bisected Adèle lifted a champagne flute at him. "Cheers."

Bentley shot upright on the bed. Adèle slept peacefully next to him, wrapped in the white linen sheets crushed from last night's sex.

As he padded barefoot to the bathroom the cold marble floor bit at his soles. The wall tiles were weeping long droplets of moisture when he stepped out of the shower, but he still felt the cold sweat on his back.

***

A week later, back in Toronto, Bentley had performed two kidney transplants and five bladder resections. Adèle finished a paper reporting her new research on gene therapy, and reviewed—and rejected—three others. They taught entitled surgical and medicine residents. They gave lectures to medical students who played with their smartphones. They attended patients in clinics and on the wards. They worked late and hardly spoke over their take-out dinners.

It was as if they both held their breath.

At home the crib grinned its slats at Bentley every time he passed the nursery they set up during the second to last pregnancy, when Adèle went beyond the twenty-week mark and they thought the pregnancy would keep. Once, when he came home from a late night in the OR, he stood outside the nursery door, his forehead against the cherry wood of the door jamb, and tried to imagine the snuffles, the mumblings of a just woken baby. But all he heard was Adele's soft breaths in the darkness of their bedroom.

Two weeks later Bentley came downstairs as Adèle stood at the kitchen counter waiting for the water to boil, teabag label hanging over the rim of her mug. He had seen the tampon wrapper and the blood-tinged applicator in the bathroom wastebasket. He reached for her, and she burrowed her face in his neck, her arms around and up his back like a vise, hands together, pushed against his spine.

Neither spoke until the kettle whistled.

"Not even a romantic interlude in Vienna," Adèle said then. Not quite how Bentley remembered it—the pickled foetuses still haunted his dreams. He reached over and poured the boiling water into the mug, dunked the teabag in and out.

"You've always taken such good care of me," Adèle said.

"I don't want a baby." He lifted her face up by the chin. "I just want you. I went along with all this, but I don't want you bloated with hormones, needles stuck in your belly, rushing off at 6 am to have an ultrasound up your hoohah."

Adèle chuckled, but a tear slid down her cheek. Bentley bent down and kissed it dry.

"We'll be all right," he said. "Just the two of us."

***

That was before the nightmares started. Before Adèle stopped going to work and just lay on the living room sofa, the pillow beneath her cheek sodden. Before Bentley was able to count the ribs beneath her disappearing muscles. And before he found her lying in a lukewarm bath, her white arms and legs floating just beneath the surface, nipples poking through the surface of the pink water, twisted wet hair snaked around her neck like a coil of umbilical cord.

But at that moment, surrounded by the aroma of the mint tea, in the orange light of the setting sun puddled on the slate tile floor, Bentley truly believed that they would be all right.

MINUS TWENTY-FIVE IN VEGREVILLE, ALBERTA

Mark Bondyra

YOU WAKE UP one cold February morning and you are in a different country.

You are lying in a blackness so complete that you can't see anything. You close your eyes and listen. You can hear your wife Marta breathing gently beside you. Is there another set of breaths there, too? Your son should be nearby, sleeping on a couch. You hear the whooshing sound of air and feel warmth washing over your face from somewhere above.

You quietly climb the basement stairs and find Tadeusz in the kitchen drinking a coffee and eating something out of a bowl. His dark brown hair is messy but the rest of his appearance is neat. He is wearing a heavy looking red and green striped shirt over a white turtleneck.

"Jacek, you're awake," he says in Polish. "Do you want some coffee?"

Outside the kitchen window it's just starting to get light. Past a small wooden patio the dark blue snow starts reaching towards a low fence. Beyond that fence is darkness and then a streak of faint orange light along the horizon.

Tadeusz pours some coffee and hands it you. You take a sip and turn the warm mug around in your hands.

"How did you sleep?"

"Good, good," you say.

"Marta and Wojtek are still asleep?"

"Yes, I think they were very tired from the trip."

Imprinted in white on the side of the mug is an egg that has been divided into a constellation of triangles. You decipher the text below the egg. It reads: 'Vegreville, the Heart of Wildrose Country.'

Vegreville, that's where you are.

When Tadeusz picked you up at the Edmonton airport last night it was dark already. You drove down an empty highway behind a snowplow until there was a thumping sound and you had to stop and change a tire that had gone flat. You and Tadeusz at the side of the highway with the cold stinging your hands and the wind blowing snow everywhere. Off in the distance you could hear a howling.

"Just coyotes," Tadeusz had said.

You take another sip of the coffee.

"Małgosia and Lucy got up early this morning to volunteer at the church. I have to take them a ham that Małgosia has been defrosting in the fridge. Will you be okay for an hour or so? Then we start planning your new life."

"Yes, no problem, don't let me keep you. I appreciate everything you're doing for us. Letting almost complete strangers stay with you like this."

"It's the good Christian thing to do. And we wouldn't be here in Canada if some family hadn't sponsored us. There's bread on the counter and eggs in the fridge, just help yourself."

Tadeusz puts his dishes in the sink and pulls a heavy coat from the hook by the door. His feet slip into big black boots.

Outside the kitchen window the burning orange ball of the sun has come up over the horizon and the sky is now radiating bands of colour. Reds, oranges and purples burst and then fade into a deep, dark blue. Beyond the fence a vast field of snow is coming into view and off in the distance something juts into the sky. It's a round silhouette against the sunrise, a ball of blackness against the reds and oranges, something human made.

You look at the thermometer attached to the outside of the window frame. The red line stops around minus twenty-five. You wonder if it's broken.

You stare out at the object on the horizon as you finish your coffee. Is it some kind of farm building?

You think about making breakfast but decide to wait until Marta and Wojtek get up. Instead you sit at the kitchen table and try to imagine what your new life in this country will look like. Where will you work? What will you do?

This town seems small, much smaller than the big cities you're used to living in. Maybe you need to go for a walk before breakfast and see what the place is like.

The army surplus jacket that you bought in West Germany hangs where Tadeusz's jacket was hanging. Next to it you see Marta's jacket—a fancy fur coat that she brought from Poland to protect her from the Canadian winter, and Wojtek's red winter coat with the white bands on the sleeves. You remember when you bought that coat and took him sledding in the park in Hamburg.

"Why did you buy that hideous thing?" Marta had said when you brought your army jacket home from the thrift shop.

"It's warm," you said. "It'll be good for our new life in Canada."

You see your boots and slip them on along with a winter hat and gloves and walk out the door.

It is stunningly cold. Every time you breathe in your nostrils stick together. You pull your zipper higher and step into the snow where footprints lead through the front yard and into the street.

Scattered throughout the yard are round snowy shapes. It is as if someone has laid a series of army helmets on the ground and waited for the snow to cover them. Or perhaps buried an entire platoon of soldiers vertically in the ground with only their helmets sticking out.

You walk to the sidewalk and look down the street. A high snow bank runs in both directions, only broken by the occasional driveway.

The sky is lighter now and has started to turn from black to a deep blue and with it the snow has started to turn white. Next door to the house is an RCMP station with two police cars parked outside. The Mounties, you think, and wonder if they also keep horses somewhere.

You choose a direction and start to walk.

You pass a barbershop. There is a wooden bar outside for tying up a horse. The kind of thing you've seen in the many Westerns that you watched while in Germany. You feel as if you have not only travelled through space but also through time to some bygone era.

Beyond the barbershop the town just ends. The road heads off to the horizon flanked on both sides by whiteness. You stand at the edge of town and see the round object off in the distance again. It does not seem to be that far away, just across the field. I have time, you think, and wander away from the road, the snow crunching when you step into it.

The cold isn't so bad, bracing. You feel alive and wonder if you'll feel like this every day now. You think about the books you read as a child. Stories set in the Canadian wilderness. The frontier. Trappers and adventurers exploring the wilds and seeking their fortunes.

The snow gets deeper, coming up over your ankles, and in places you even plunge in up to your knee. When you look back you see your trail of footprints travelling back towards the edge of town. The wind starts to blow across your bare face and the last streaks of orange and red disappear leaving behind a piercing blue sky. In the distance you see the round object again. It sparkles as the sunlight hits it.

You can feel the cold getting into your hands and feet and you think about how bulky Tadeusz's boots were. You try to pull your jacket zipper higher but it's as high as it will go so you pull your hat lower over your ears and trudge ahead.

Sitting in your friend's apartment in Germany with Marta and Wojtek you remember discussing whether to return to Poland or to try and emigrate to Canada. To a better life.

For months things had been getting worse in Poland. Threats of strikes. Long line-ups for food. People were being called up to the army. A man came to your apartment every day looking for you, saying you needed to report for service.

And every day Marta would say that she hadn't seen you. That you had been gone for weeks. This was not so uncommon in Poland, husbands just leaving wives, just walking out. There was even a joke about it.

"Where's your husband, Miss?"

"Oh, he just stepped out to get the paper ... a week ago."

For some reason you now find this joke hilarious. You feel happy that you managed to leave. That you managed to strike some small victory against the communists that had wormed their way into every aspect of your life. Staying would have meant the army and the expectation that you would be willing to turn against your own countrymen to support a regime you did not believe in.

With every step your feet plunge through the snow's crust and the hard edge of it bumps against your shins. Your breath comes harder now, more ragged. You decide that the thermometer outside the kitchen window had indeed been correct.

The wind gusts, a cold and biting thing that picks up the snow and obscures your vision. The round object in the distance has gotten a little bigger and a little rounder. You can see now that it's not attached to the ground. It's somehow hovering in midair, suspended there by some unknown force.

You wiggle your toes inside your boots and try walking faster to generate some heat. You plunge your feet forward one step after another and then you decide to try running.

The crust bangs harder against your shins as you plough ahead until your right foot catches and you fall forward, landing face first in the snow.

You lie there out of breath for a moment feeling the cold.

Maybe it's time to turn back. You stand up and look back towards where you came from but everything has disappeared in the blowing snow. You can see a short distance and then there is just an impenetrable blanket of white.

You consider the possibility that you might freeze to death on your first day in Canada and that the police will find your frozen body here in the middle of the prairie.

"*No, jesteś taki głupi,*" you can hear Marta saying to you.

You're so stupid.

Marta doesn't speak English and the prospect of leaving her alone in this new country fills you with terror. You wonder if you can follow your footprints back but already you can see them filling with snow. Your lone reference point is now the round object which keeps appearing and disappearing with every wind gust.

You walk faster. As fast as you can without falling over. You can't feel your feet or fingers now.

Everything goes silent and you hear only the sound of your feet on the snow and the wind.

Over your shoulder you see the glowing orb of the sun. You try to remember your training in the Polish army, back in your wilderness navigation course. It's simple. If you keep the sun in the same position you should be able to travel in a straight enough line. And if you keep travelling in a straight enough line you will reach the round object.

And if you don't you will probably walk around in a circle until you find your own footprints and then you will probably die. This idea fills your chest and stomach with red hot terror.

You keep walking. You put one foot in front of the other and just keep walking and then for a moment the wind drops and you can see the object. You have veered to the right and are no longer walking straight towards it but from your new vantage point you can see that it's an egg. A giant egg hovering above the ground.

You correct your course as the egg once again disappears from view and you hope that you are still heading towards it.

You think you can hear cars and that perhaps the highway is close by, that perhaps someone will pick you up.

When the egg finally comes back into view you can see that it's actually standing on a thin triangular base. You see a pattern of gold and silver and brown on its surface that turns into a series of repeating triangles as you get closer.

And suddenly it's obvious.

You remember the mug. The object in the distance with its triangular patterns is the egg that was on the side of the mug.

You are close enough now that you can hear the wind howling around the egg and as you approach you realize that it's huge.

It looks futuristic. It seems to be made up of a series of different coloured metals and it hovers above you and for a moment you forget you are cold. You slip your glove off and stand up to touch the bottom of the egg. The metal freezes your hand and quickly you put your glove back on and stand there shivering. Now that you have stopped you are losing body heat with every gust of the wind.

You do some jumping jacks to try and get some warm blood flowing into your hands and feet, which have gone completely numb. There is nothing but whiteness all around you and now you're not even sure which direction you came from.

You're afraid to walk away from the egg because you fear losing your only reference point.

Out of breath but a bit warmer you stop doing the jumping jacks and then you hear it. A car engine, somewhere not too far away. Your lowered hands start to sting painfully as the warm blood flows back into them.

You don't want to leave the little shelter that the egg offers but you know you can't stay here. You step into the white void and head towards the sound.

When the sound recedes you stop walking and turn around to make sure that you can still see the egg.

You listen. Waiting.

It is there again, the sound of an engine. You walk and noise gets louder and then drifts away. There is a road somewhere in the whiteness.

You hear another car and you run towards the sound until it disappears. You stop again. Every time you stop a little more heat leaks out of your body.

Minutes pass and you begin to shiver.

And then you hear a deeper rumble and see two glowing suns moving through the blanket of snow.

You run and see a snow bank and a red set of taillights and then your foot catches on the snow crust and you fall straight down hitting the snow bank hard with your chest and face.

You lie there out of breath and feel the coldness spreading. Maybe if you just close your eyes, just for a minute, you will have the energy to stand up. You listen to your heart thudding in your chest.

You don't know how long you have been lying there when you hear a rumble followed by the sound of a door opening and closing.

"Hey, you okay?"

You lift your head and see a man in a cowboy hat. Behind him is a dirty red truck with a snowplow on the front.

"You need help?"

"I'm very cold," you say.

"Where's your car?"

"I was walking," you point into the blizzard.

"You walked? From where? From town? In this weather?"

The man puts his hand under your arm and lifts you up. He looks you up and down and brushes the snow off your jacket.

"Well, come on, get in the pick-up," he says.

You open the passenger door and see two rifles in the back window. It is warm. The cowboy flips a switch on the dashboard and hot air blasts out at you.

The man is older, maybe in his early fifties.

"My name's Stan," he says, reaching his hand out.

"Jacek," you say, shaking his hand.

"Jacek. You French or something?"

"Polish," you say.

"Oh, Polish. Lots of Ukrainians around here, but I've never met a Polish guy," he says. "What were you doing walking in the snow?"

"I want to see egg," you say, pointing.

"The Pysanka? Yeah—it's like an Easter egg, the biggest one in the world."

"Pysanka, yes, I know this word, it's the same word in Polish."

Stan drives slowly down the highway. You can barely see out of the windshield and are surprised when you discover that you have driven back into town and are crawling down the main street past the Canadian Tire.

Stan stops the truck in front of your house and shakes your hand again.

"You take care, Jacek."

You walk back through the snowy yard into the house where your wife and child are still sleeping soundly in the basement.

THE DULCIMER GIRL

Norman Ravvin

1.

THE OFFER ARRIVES by e-mail. Life-changing surprises come this way, at a glance. The note is signed, *Lusia Wiespolska,* under the address Lewandowska Pictures. Warsaw, *ulica* Sienna 42/46. It reads:

Dear Nadia Baltzan,

We have had word of your lovely way with the dulcimer. We are at a loss here. The whole of Poland will not cough up a player who can make your instrument do what we need it to do. Our mutual friend Simon Hanover directed me to a You-Tube film of you. You are playing Mary Hopkins. As they say in poems: my heart is broken. Thankfully, you are not viral. You are our own little secret. The Dulcimer Girl. Let us know if you accept from Lewandowska Pictures:

    1.)   first class air-fare Vancouver-Frankfurt-Warsaw return

    2.)   driver to Radzanów for one day shoot, return

    3.)   downtown Warsaw recording location with recording engineer Jacek Uchman, who has worked with Tomasz Stańko

    4.)   accomm. Warsaw Old Town, Hotel Regina

    5.)   payment $500 US/day including travel days

Details of the film we are shooting appear on our web site. It is historical.

If you are willing, I will forward dates and flights, which are booked and await you and your instrument. I have informed

the airline that the dulcimer must not be taken from you. They will likely inspect it in weird secure backrooms. (I experienced this when another project required a costume from an Italian museum, which had been worn by a compatriot of Marie Antoinette!) I await your hopefully agreeable response.
  Yours from Poland,
  Lusia Wiespolska

It seems unreal. It reminds her of fake emails that arrive offering an escrow account of £45 million. *The Emir of Zuru would like to inform you that you are his long lost descendant, sole heir to his castles, his gold mines, his stock of Scottish malt liquor.*
  But Simon Hanover is in fact an acquaintance, someone Nadia used to see in music clubs around Vancouver.
  She replies: "Sure. I'm your Dulcimer Girl."

2.

Nadia thinks of the ruins back home in Vancouver. She holds them in her mind's eye as her plane crosses the Atlantic: Hotel Balmoral, with its blind clock; the Hotel Empress, its windows frosted with tinfoil; the Regent Hotel—once among the street's substantial buildings. A hundred years before, the Fisherman's Union ran its business out of the Regent, encroached upon now by a gaping construction hole. The Hazelwood Hotel, woe to the sad Hazelwood, with its stained brick-front and haphazardly repaired door. Across the road, the Patricia, with its refurbished sign hanging over the sidewalk, theatre style. At night, she guessed, if you left your curtains open, the neon would colour a darkened room, cinematic and scary.
  These were her ruins and she loved them in her way. Included among them was the weirdly razor-wired gate across the gaping space where her father's brother had tendered loans to the ruined

men of Hastings and Cordova. This is where he received a head-bashing, a fight on his knees for his life. She felt pleased and a little proud that she'd stood inside that ruin, too. Even if it had been re-purposed as an upscale boutique called WANT. Whenever she walked by she thought to herself: What do I want?

To think about these things she needs music, so she slips on her headphones and reaches into her bag to start "Sweet Jane," performed so the listener can appreciate every drum tap, each slide of the guitarist's fingers on the strings, and the singer's whispery voice:

> *You're waiting for Jimmy*
> *Down in the alley.*
> *You're waiting for him to come back home.*

3.

Lusia Wiespolska has performed her job flawlessly. Nadia gazes at what was done atop the ruins of Warsaw's lovely Old Town, its purposeful reconstruction in the 1950s. She knows nothing about European architecture, so she cannot appreciate which era each stuccoed villa is meant to imitate. Her guidebook makes it clear: everything here was destroyed by the Germans during the Warsaw Uprising.

This morning, beginning at dawn, she walked from a hill over-looking the Vistula, back toward the *Rynek Nowego Miasta*, the square near her hotel, then on to the Barbican, the remains of the city's fortress gate. In the distance she glimpsed the spires of a gigantic church, then further along, a glittering sports stadium. Both of these were beyond the river, in Praga. She used her guidebook to consider how long it would take to walk, but realized there wasn't time. So she headed back along Kościelna to Freta, taking in each roof dormer, every shift in the cobblestone detail, the delicate glass and iron fixtures telling street number and name. It was early enough as she walked that few people were out. She stared without fearing she looked like a tourist.

In the *Rynek Nowego Miasta* no one is out but her. Umbrellas, shut tight over café tables, await the day's customers. Pigeons congregate on granite steps. She'd done well to get up early, to see what she could before the driver was due to take her to the film shoot north of the city. No one had said anything about what to wear, so she is in her usual outfit, jeans and a t-shirt, along with an old pair of black hiking boots. They are comfortable and promote walking. *Keep on going,* they seem to say. *We're not done yet.*

Through the glass doorway of what looks like a Renaissance church she watches a nun, her black habit loose on her forehead, rearrange pamphlets on a tabletop. Their eyes meet and Nadia thinks, I must get back.

The hotel is fronted by a series of arcades, just off the sidewalk. White tablecloths flap in the breeze. She listens for a moment to a bird call—is it an owl? In an e-mail, the driver had insisted he would find her inside the lobby. Nadia takes the stairs up to her room to collect her dulcimer. She returns and settles onto one of the gigantic white sofas that dominate the lobby. Opposite her sits a man with closely trimmed grey hair. Something about him—his age?— makes her think he is a traveller on his way to the royal castle to see the Rembrandts. With the instrument case between her knees she awaits her pickup.

The man looks at the case and nods in greeting. He says: "Please."
Nadia shrugs. What does he mean?
"*Proszę.* Play your *cymbał.*" He crosses his arms.
Nadia opens the case, takes her instrument out and begins to play. The acoustics are fine. Her audience of one smiles and closes his eyes. She can hear him breathing softly, in a kind of meditative response to the music. Nadia plays one of the Polish-Jewish pieces she suggested to Lusia Wiespolska when she'd agreed to come. Before her departure she practiced it so many times she plays it with complete ease, and thinks as she does about adding what are, in her

mind, little Polish touches. The riffs and details she hopes will please the film people.

It will be a new experience to play for money. This has never been her modus operandi. She received her university scholarship in order to *think* about music. She appeared on little rickety Vancouver stages for open mic nights because these were entirely anonymous surroundings. She thinks of what she's read about the Polish fiddle, the *suka*, which gains its timbre by the player stopping its strings with his fingernails. She cannot play like this on her dulcimer, but she aspires to such playing, an old-time, *kapela* feeling, in the hope that this will be expressed in her song.

She notices a man by the lobby door. He wears a dark suit, sunglasses, and one of those Bluetooth pieces in his ear. He must be her driver. She lets the song run its course and puts her instrument back in its case. The man opposite, her listener, stands. He holds his arms wide and she steps into them as he hugs her.

"I have not heard anything like this in a long time," he says. "The real Polish music." His response confirms that she will give the filmmakers what they want. She can relax and let it all happen.

The driver holds the lobby door for her and then opens the rear door of a long black car. She falls into the back seat with the dulcimer beside her. Once the driver has taken his seat, he looks over his shoulder and says: "Radzanów. One hour." And they are off to the countryside.

4.

Nadia cannot read the landscape. It is well-tended, punctuated by distant forests. The driver does not address her, as if she were a visiting dignitary and *must not be bothered*. This makes her smile. She is the only person in the world who can play Polish-Jewish music in a way that pleases the director of a wartime drama.

They approach Radzanów on a road that curves through trees.

They pass an old wooden church. The village appears around a bend in the road and takes shape upon a central square. On one side, a large white church with its wedding cake steeple. Decrepit wooden buildings. Newish stucco two-storey homes and much older brick houses. The sky above is the lightest blue. The driver turns his head as they roll to a stop. He says: "Radzanów, market square." Nadia gets out to stretch. The car pulls away. Along the roadway comes a group of men and women. Out front is a young woman. She reaches for Nadia's hand to pull her close.

"Hi. I'm Lusia? You're right on time. Witold is reliable behind the wheel of the Skoda."

The rest of the group keeps their distance. One studies a clipboard. Another talks into a cell phone. It is Lusia's job to welcome her, to make sure that the expensive visiting musician from Canada does her job well and is sent on to Warsaw.

"We have," Lusia explains, "one scene to do. It takes place in a nearby meadow, with no one in sight but you. The rest of what we need you for takes place in the studio tomorrow. Is that okay?"

Nadia nods. For what they are paying her this is an acceptable plan.

"Great." Lusia nudges her in the direction of the others. "We have a short walk. It's easier than roaring up in a vehicle." They take a dirt road through what looks like a farmer's back property. The village falls away behind them as the flat land, the church spire, and a low brick building become the only things in view.

They cross fields and meadows. Soft humps and gullies are marked by fence posts hewn from boughs. In the distance a scattering of trees. Behind these an escarpment, a rough blue shoulder against the sky.

"So. Here." Lusia motions at a coat rack where a black jacket and a pair of pants hang.

"There's a belt if they're too big." Lusia leads her to what looks like a big outhouse but turns out to be a makeshift changing room. Nadia pulls the door shut behind her. She takes off her boots and pants and puts on the black clothes. A belt is fitted into the costume pants, long enough for her to tighten in a knot. She sits on a low stool in the corner to tie up her boots. A pair of shoes sit along the wall, but her boots look fine with the rest of what's been set out. A fedora with a copper-coloured band and a blue feather hangs on a hook on the back of the door. She tucks her hair inside its crown and pulls the hat down over her brow. Who, she wonders, is she dressed as? Estragon from *Waiting for Godot*? A Polish circus clown? She takes the dulcimer out of its case and steps into the midday sun.

"Okay?" Lusia points to a chair that sits on a rise in the meadow some twenty metres off. "You sit there. We'll film from the back, and with that"—she points at a raised platform—"from above as well. The chair is miked. In Warsaw we'll have you play the same piece in case we need a fill."

"What is this field?" Nadia wonders aloud as the camera people fiddle and jostle with their equipment.

Lusia glances at her. "We needed something, you know, unpeopled. With a good view into the distance." She waves at the trees, the escarpment, the cloudless sky. They walk toward the chair. Nadia settles herself on it.

"We need you," Lusia says, "to be still when you play."

Nadia places her heels firmly in the grass and gets her instrument in place, mid-thigh, to feel the right looseness. She gives the strings a strum.

Lusia hovers in Nadia's peripheral view and then is gone.

Gazing into the distance Nadia wonders if she will ever again play music in so strange a setting.

"So?" Lusia is back. "Ready?"

Nadia nods. Her song is titled *Rumanische Fantasien.* Of the recordings she sent as possibilities, it is the one that fit the filmmaker's idea of a Jewish-Polish song. Or a Polish-Jewish song, depending on who it was she corresponded with. Lusia had written to say she thought Nadia played like "an old Polish bluesman." The director could not believe the person playing was a girl. "BURN THIS AFTER

READING," Lusia wrote, "CAN YOU BELIEVE HE SAID THAT?" She lays a light hand on Nadia's shoulder and speaks quietly. "When I've backed away, count sixty. Then play. You won't be aware of us at all. The camera guy will be able to shift his depth of field, so we'll bring you in close, in your old gypsy suit. Okay?"

Nadia nods. Once Lusia is out of view she counts, from sixty to ten, slowing herself at four, three, two, one ... and moves into the slow repetition of the song's first chords. A bird calls and she takes this as her cue to shift into the quicker pace at the centre of the song, a whirl of rhythm four times as fast as the rest, which might have once given dancers at a wedding what they needed to propel the bride, up, on a rickety chair. Then back to the slow march, in order for the song to return to its beginning point. It's a song that could go on forever, in and out of fast and slow sections.

As she concludes, Nadia listens to the way the dulcimer sounds on the meadow. She nears the song's final movement and a crazy thing happens. In the near distance, by a line of fence posts, a figure appears, bent over at first, then upright, carrying something under her arm. The figure comes closer and Nadia sees that it is a woman. Old and stout. She carries a basket under one arm. Her hair is white against the greens and browns of the countryside. She stops and listens. This is a distraction, but Nadia winds the song up without a hitch. She sits still, hands on the dulcimer's strings. The crew begins to grumble and call in Polish.

"That was great!" Lusia rushes by, heading toward the woman in the field. Nadia watches as they talk. Then the old woman walks off toward town, and Lusia makes her way back. "That was beautiful. The crew loved it. That"—she points at the old woman heading down the road—"we didn't expect. But we're going with it. A little local flavour. Okay?"

Nadia nods.

"Listen. Our driver has to leave at five. Is that alright? You'll be back early and you can grab a good dinner at the hotel. You'll be rested and ready for the studio tomorrow."

Nadia re-enters the makeshift dressing room. She hangs the jacket, pants and hat on the hook on the back of the plywood door. By the time she is outside, dressed as herself again, the crew has packed up. With Lusia she makes her way toward the village.

"Are you hungry?" Lusia rummages around in a white plastic bag. "Craft services left us these. Sandwiches. A salad. I have coffee."

The idea of the back seat of the chauffeured car on an empty stomach makes Nadia feel sick. They eye a stump, a couple feet wide, off the rutted road, and sit. Lusia sets out what she has on the stump and they gaze across the sandy ground at the church in the distance. Its wedding cake tiers sparkle in the sunlight. Nadia is happy for the break. The coffee tastes almost fresh.

"This is a very peaceful spot."

Lusia leans back, pulling a cigarette from a shirt pocket. "Sure."

"How long have you been filming here?"

"We took over the place for a few weeks. The planning took longer. I'm a Radzanów expert. The only one in the world under seventy-five."

"Where does my scene fit?"

"Well. You're the music. When we record tomorrow you'll put down a lot of what we'll use on the soundtrack."

"No. I mean the scene you just shot. The old woman. What was she doing?"

"She said, collecting."

"Collecting what?"

"Jewish herbs. *Żydowskie zioła.*" Lusia hesitates. "Before the war that meadow was a graveyard." She sighs, for the first time less than bristling with enthusiasm. "It's a long story. I could get you a copy of the script."

Nadia feels uneasy at the thought of her name appearing in the film's credits. The meadow, its backdrop, the apparition of the woman walking into the scene. It all seems unlikely to her as they picnic by a farmer's castoff stuff—spare tractor parts and tires in a neat totem.

She looks toward the town.

Lusia brushes herself off.

They point themselves toward the village. Nadia wonders, but not out loud, about the distant mountains, the trees and the meadow where a bird signals where you are in your song.

THE TRUTH TO TELL

Pamela Mulloy

IF THEY'D ALLOWED the truth there was much to tell. That Jacek was buying shares in a farm outside Warsaw, but worried about his evasive partners; that Katherine believed she was pregnant but was too afraid to find out; that Beata still held dreams of doing a doctorate in history because she was bright, though she concealed it well; and that, despite the troubles at the Agency, Peter was thinking of settling in Poland permanently.

"These meetings. They're killing me," Jacek said, rubbing his neck as if representing the agricultural sector matched a day behind a tiller.

"Seven hours today and nothing accomplished." Katherine set her beer on the table and slid next to him.

Things had started to fall apart months ago. Rumours began that the President at the Foreign Investment Agency would be sacked, that others would follow. There was money involved. Lots of it. This in the name of progress since the Wall had come down two years earlier. Western governments wanted to give the Agency money, but not until the Ministry of Privatization approved a plan. The plan was proving elusive and troublesome, and so their team of four had been assembled.

Peter and Beata sat with their drinks, her hand on his knee while he leaned back, arms stretched out along the back of the banquette in the newly opened English pub.

"I heard that someone from the Ministry is expected again tomorrow," Jacek said. "We need a plan they can live with."

"It's the money they want, not a plan," Beata said. "Don't be blind."

"Selective blindness can be useful." Jacek tilted his glass to her.

For weeks, pockets of staff, secretaries, managers, and even the foreign consultants had gathered in the Agency speculating about their future. The *real* problem was that the Ministry wanted the money for *their* needs but did not know how to wrench it from the Agency. Delegates from the Ministry had started showing up for meetings with the President. Then a week ago the Minister himself arrived, prompting the underlings at the Agency to scatter like marbles. Those trapped in his presence were left holding open doors. After that, the President spent most days alone in his office, waiting. Only Peter was allowed to see him. It was Katherine who later discovered the intent of these meetings.

"It's the same bloody thing, history repeats itself while the country stargazes," Jacek said.

"You're a fucking poet, Jacek," Peter said.

Katherine looked at Peter, who had disappeared into his beer glass. "We need a break," she announced.

"Patience, Katherine. This can't go on forever."

"It's already been forever."

There had been the illusion of progress in the past few weeks; and then a different sort of rumour began to emerge. A familiar pattern, almost an expectation for those with long memories. Accusations about misappropriation of funds. Careless spending. Insinuations of wrongdoings. The Minister didn't really need an excuse to remove the President, but specific charges would give the dismissal credence.

"A few days away would do us good," Katherine said.

"We can go to Łańcut," Beata suggested, looking at Peter, then Katherine. "I went there as a child. There's a castle."

"We can leave on Friday," Katherine said.

"But I have a meeting," Peter protested.

"Cancel it," Jacek said. "Nothing will happen without you."

The next day Katherine went to the tourist office for a map, Jacek picked up a book on the history of Łańcut Castle, Beata booked the rooms, and Peter attended more meetings.

***

It was the first time the four of them had travelled together and they were still unsure of each other's stress points. They'd been working together at the Agency for nine months now, helping Polish and foreign companies manoeuvre from the collapse of communism into the nascent rules of Western multinational capitalism. Beata and Jacek, both Project Managers, were the first generation to see a future in Poland since the exit of the Soviets a few years earlier. Beata was ambitious, but for what she was still unsure. Jacek had an air of contentment about him—a radical father, once arrested for setting up the Thursday Club, a meeting place for writers who published abroad, and an alcoholic mother had made him adept at accepting his lot. Peter, from the UK, and Katherine, a Canadian, civil servants both, had been sent to the Agency by their respective governments to offer a "Western" perspective on the changes.

Though Beata was the one who suggested Łańcut, once there she began to pine for home. The season was all wrong, she decided, the splendour of autumn having given way to pre-winter. There'd been high expectations: a weekend that would wipe away the strain they'd all been under, allow them a new level of connection. That it wasn't as immediately vibrant or bountiful as they'd hoped, now seemed a personal insult. Beata blamed Peter's bland enthusiasm, as if it could somehow infect weather patterns, landscapes, the intensity of friendships.

"We shouldn't have come," Beata said, as they pulled into the town eyeing the plaster-clad buildings, soot-grey with years of neglect, hand painted signs—*Apteka, Cukiernia, Delikatesy*—alongside one gleaming Coca-Cola advertisement. She sighed. "It looks like Łańcut has not heard about capitalism." Although she was well-practiced at holding her tongue, melodrama was her true skill.

At breakfast the next morning Peter was waiting for them at the café. Katherine joined him a half hour later. Beata abhorred the morning, but Peter was intent on an early start, and he'd convinced the others that after the six-hour drive the day before they should take full advantage of the place. Now they felt rushed, and Beata was irritable, the idea of a relaxed weekend quickly dissipating. After all, there were no plans other than going to the castle at some point. There was little else to do in this town on the southeast edge of Poland.

"Go on without me," Beata said, still half asleep. She sat staring into her coffee, Peter forcing a menu on her.

"We'll walk the grounds first," Jacek said. Peter shot him a look, and Katherine only shrugged her assent.

The castle was originally constructed in 1629 for Stanisław Lubormirski, the major landowner of the region, as a fortress-type residence with donjons in each corner surrounded by fortifications. Jacek had been reading about the castle and was eager to share his newfound knowledge.

"When Izabella Lubomirska lived in Poland she used to send her laundry to Paris," Jacek announced, proudly.

"That is not history," Beata said.

She withdrew her hand from Peter's and sat fidgeting with her coffee cup, the spoon clattering against the saucer. Peter gazed at two women out front of the café walking to the castle annex where Beata had booked their rooms for the weekend.

"They will be cleaning our rooms," he said quietly. "I left my passport."

Jacek waved him off. "What would they do with your passport? You are too ugly. No one would claim to be you." They laughed at this, but Peter's look of rebuke soon quieted them.

"Foreign passports don't have the same value now," Beata said, glancing at Jacek, who'd once told her that his journalist grand-father had helped a friend obtain a passport through unofficial channels so that he could leave the country for a conference. The friend smuggled a copy of *Dr. Zhivago* back to Poland and gave it to Jacek's father. Jacek still owned it, although it remained unread. He had no patience for fiction.

Beata was absently worrying the corner of a brochure she'd pulled from her bag while Peter went back to watching the cleaning women, their hair dyed rust-red.

"They told us to be careful of our passports," he said.

"Oh, did *they*?" Jacek raised an eyebrow to Beata, who reached out as if to calm Peter.

Peter and Beata had been seeing each other for three months now, but publicly only for the last six weeks. They had not reached the point where they could talk of a future.

"Let's get the bill." Katherine rose from her chair, her hand touching Jacek's shoulder as she walked past, thinking about the baby, wondering if she should talk to him about it this weekend. Beata stood, her chair scraping loudly across the floor, and headed for the door. The others followed.

***

They walked down the centre of the town, pausing at a shop to admire a display of children's clothes held up by strings like stretched animal hides, then continued on past two Fiats parked on the road —one red, one white, both badly dented.

"That one's like your *maluch*," Peter said, squeezing Beata's shoulder, but she shrugged him off, running her fingernails along the red car as she walked by.

They side-stepped a queue of women waiting for bread at the *piekarina* in the otherwise abandoned street. A cockerel crowed, then a dog responded furiously. The sun had not yet burned through the clouds and this added to the dampness so pervasive it made their clothes feel wet.

At the castle, they strolled along the edge of the grassy moat. Peter and Beata went ahead while Katherine, with a hand resting absently on her belly, trailed Jacek, who kept referring to the guidebook as if they were lost. They were aimless in their wandering, past the vine-draped pergola and the skeleton of climbing roses up the wall of the orangery, along the path near the coach house that held more than eighty horse-drawn carriages. The Palace itself, under Lubomirska's guidance, had been transformed from the original solid fortress into a style following the late eighteenth century trend in Classicism, with an emphasis on symmetry, proportion, and geometry.

"*When living abroad, Lubomirska purchased many sculptures, paintings and artifacts and amassed enormous collections of vases and classical sculptures, most of which now are in the residence in Łańcut.*" Jacek lowered the guidebook and looked to the others.

"It was the fashion of that period to create buildings that were cultural and political symbols, as well as works of art," Beata said.

"Let's go inside," Katherine said. "I'm cold."

The wind scooped up a cluster of leaves and sent them wheeling across the drive. Hunched in their jackets, Jacek and Katherine headed to the castle entrance, the other two trailed behind. Inside, their footsteps, led by the hard heels of Katherine's boots, alerted the security guard, who looked up from his newspaper as if he'd been interrupted in an involved clerical task. They paid admission and entered a world that instantly eclipsed the one they'd left behind.

They made their way along the corridor, taking in the curvature of the ceilings, the alabaster sculptures, breezing past paintings of past residents, each canvas dim, some bearing hairline cracks from age. They walked softly now, as if silence was a rarity that must be preserved, and entered the library, which, with its billiard table, leather furnishings and collection of 22,000 books that lined the walls, resembled an English gentlemen's club.

"I don't know that I could live here," Beata said with a note of disdain.

Jacek sniffed, glanced at Beata, and was about to mention the reality of her living space in Warsaw—two ten-by-ten-foot rooms she shared with her mother in a pre-fab concrete, communist-era flat—but then thought better of it.

"*In 1785 she became involved in the so-called Dogrumowa affair, a sex and murder scandal that rocked her family, and after losing the case, left Poland never to return."* Jacek looked up, checking to make sure that they were still listening.

"There is something wrong with all this opulence when down the road people are starving," Katherine said, hooking her hand into Jacek's arm. "It's the same, even today."

"You are too practical," Jacek said. "The solutions are never easy. Anyway, Izabela loved beautiful things, but she took care of the people in the villages of her estate. They had schools, doctors, mid-wives."

"History repeats itself to a fault." Katherine freed herself from Jacek and walked away.

"The past is all we have, it's who we are, all we've ever been," Jacek said, slamming the guidebook onto the billiard table near Katherine.

"The truth of it is, she's right," Beata said as she and Peter exited the room, heading for the ballroom.

Katherine turned her back to Jacek, her hand gliding across the books on the shelf.

"Why did we come here?" Katherine asked.

"It was supposed to be good for us," Jacek said.

"Us? Is there an us?"

***

When Jacek and Katherine entered the grand ballroom, Beata and Peter, who were in an embrace at the centre of the room, shifted into an exaggerated waltz, swooping across the floor.

"Come on. Join us," Peter called out, but Katherine waved them off, announcing that she was going to the dining room. Jacek went to the threshold of the adjoining rooms, and began moving back and forth, looking intently at the floor as if he'd lost something.

"Come. Look," he said to Katherine. He stopped at the doorway that led to the dining room then, dropping to his knees, ran one hand over the design. "Each floor is unique." On all fours, he traced the lines with his finger. Then he sat back on his heels and looked across the dining room at the elaborate marquetry of the oak floor, which resembled rows of spun rope pieced together from contrasting dark and light wood. "Look at this," he said. "Now, this is a plan."

Katherine stood nearby, watching him straddle the entrance of the corridor and dining room, looking at the semblance of ropes on one floor, and the combination of geometric and plant-inspired motifs, like elaborate boxed-in rosettes, in the other.

"Up close, it's simple. Dark wood against light, the shapes put together for contrast. But the vision, that's genius."

Jacek reached out to Katherine's hand for her to pull him up from the floor, and slung his arm around her clumsily.

"Maybe none of it matters," Jacek said, gazing out across the room. "All of the nonsense at the Agency. Perspective. That's what we have to think about."

They walked into the dining room, their footsteps placed carefully as they followed the rope pattern. Something had loosened in them, a tautness or sense of responsibility, an affectation they'd acquired in their months working together.

This was the artfulness of the place, the opulence a kind of erasure.

"It's good that we came after all," Jacek said. "Just for this alone."

"Peter's right, Jacek. You are a fucking poet."

***

"*Isabella founded a distillery here, specializing in anise flavoured vodka.*" Jacek was leaning against the doorframe in the vestibule when Beata and Peter caught up with them.

"Then we should drink to her." Beata held up her hand as if raising a glass.

Peter hooked his hand into Beata's elbow and led her out the door.

"I don't understand her," Katherine said. They were watching Beata kiss Peter on the cheek as they descended the stairs. "You know her father imports Korean televisions?"

"What does that matter?"

"They have money."

Jacek walked on.

Outside, the bracing autumn air seemed a relief, the snarl of brittle leaves underfoot breaking the silence as Katherine and Jacek walked across the courtyard.

Jacek looked back at the castle. He stood for a few moments before joining the others, who were leaning against a stony ledge.

"After a failed plot to kill the king, Madame Dogrumova turned her attention to Izabela's husband, the Grand Marshall. There was false poison, which was eventually discovered to be an aphrodisiac, spies hiding in cupboards, Izabela's family publicly humiliated after being set up by this harlot who claimed she'd been asked to seduce, then poison him by those in power."

"We should have such excitement in our lives," Beata said. "We go back and forth like minions each day."

"There are many ways to be happy." Jacek looked over to her then continued: *"She was indignant; she turned her back on Poland after the scandal."*

"To put energy into decorating this place and never live here." Katherine was fixated on this, the seemingly wasted extravagance.

"We are all drawn to pretty things." Peter was twirling a strand of Beata's hair.

"But she ran away, she turned her back on Poland." Beata paced in front of the others. "She drew an enormous sum from her estate while living abroad."

"But this is her legacy, she left something beautiful behind. She had a vision." Jacek was getting agitated again. "And you call *me* blind."

"Come on, let's walk along the river," Peter said.

***

They ate dinner in the same restaurant in which they'd had break-fast. *Bigos, pierogi, schnitzel.* Then they bought wine and drank it sitting on the floor of Jacek's room.

"I don't want to lose my job." Beata was a little drunk.

"Beata, we made a promise," Peter said.

"Fuck the promise." Then she smiled. "Now you can tell me about fairness." They all knew Peter's position was safe. He had a foreign contract.

"Perhaps I'll go to Paris," Jacek said.

Katherine looked at him as if he might be serious. "You don't speak French."

"What does it matter? I'll find a Polish company. I have experi-ence."

"I could go to Canada," Beata said. "I have an aunt there."

"We said we wouldn't talk about this," Katherine said.

The room became stuffy and eventually someone got up to open a window. The moon drew a silhouette over Łańcut, the curvature of the cupola on the castle tower like a lantern amongst the stars. They sat listening to the stillness, waiting for something to happen.

If they'd allowed the truth, there was much to say. That Beata's father was indeed making money but had abandoned the family and she was left supporting her mother and sister; that most nights Jacek sat alone in the flat his parents had left him, both long dead, and his job was something he clung to, the only thing that gave him a sense of belonging; that Peter was once a rising star back in the UK until a reshuffling left him out of a job, and so he'd reinvented himself as a consultant; that Katherine had left behind a fiancé who was unaware they would never marry. They were outliers, friends of a sort, and this weekend was meant to take them away from their lives, but the setting, the mood, left them each locked in their own circumstances.

"*Haughty and challenging in contacts with persons close to her, Izabela treated Polish affairs with indifference. She died in Vienna.*"

"Shut up, Jacek," Beata said, leaning into him.

"Don't be rude, Beata." Peter got up, staggering a bit as he reached for the cigarettes in his jacket.

Katherine watched Peter for a moment. He was drunk, she saw, and she worried that he might confess to something he would regret tomorrow. It was Peter who'd been tasked with forming a list of who should be let go if the Agency President was fired. It was he, in his private meetings with the President, who drew up recommendations based on areas of need. They did not require so many in the agricultural sector; retail, too, was overstaffed. Katherine had seen the list later, when she'd met with the President. Beata and Jacek's names were both there. Katherine had not spoken to Peter about the list. This weekend they'd all made a vow not to talk about the troubles.

She wanted to be angry with Peter, but felt only pity, for she knew that he was as lost as anyone else in the room. She reached the wine bottle toward Jacek's glass. He had gone quiet, barely aware that she was there.

"And what will you do, Peter? If the Ministry pulls the plug?" Jacek asked, looking up abruptly.

"I will do as the Ministry sees fit," he said, striking a match, knowing he had no other choice.

PAPER ICON

Robert B. Young

SABINA PRAYED. ON her chest, a cross pendant gleamed in the sunlight streaming through the office window. She hadn't slept properly for days, and she told herself, it's the summer heat. The humidity. But she knew the cause: that second *Past Due* notice, which had stared out from her mailbox.

Bill came in with two coffees and closed the office door. As he sat down at his desk, the name tag on his shirt flashed the sun into Sabina's eyes. She had left the top three buttons of her blouse undone, and the cross hung just above her cleavage. Since Borys, she had eschewed perfume, but for this meeting she wore Esteé Lauder to mask the cigarette smell. She hated acting in this play.

"I'm sorry," Bill said. He raked his fingers through grey hair. "But the mortgage papers you signed are quite clear about default. You've missed two payments in a row. And one last year and another the year before. So unfortunate. You and Borys were such good clients."

When Borys was a young construction worker, he had swaggered on the Częstochowa streets, and Sabina had loved his muscles and tanned neck. But he had died a fat, flaccid man. Bill, who was over six feet tall, was her age yet still fit.

The traffic hummed beyond the window. Stratford had a split personality: half farm town, half Shakespearean festival. Fanning themselves in the heat, tourists hurried to make the two-o'clock showtime at the festival's downtown theatres. Flatbed trucks loaded with I-beams and John Deere tractors clattered by. Dodge Caravans and Honda Odysseys, packed with vacationers, honked as they squeezed past each other. Among the Ontario licenses, cars sported plates from Quebec, Michigan, New York, or Pennsylvania.

Sabina remembered taking summer road trips with her two young daughters and Borys, not long after leaving Poland. But her daughters had matured in what seemed like ten minutes and had left Stratford; the house had become bleak during the day. So she'd volunteered for the festival and taken some of its acting workshops as a refresher. She found the courses disappointing. No sense of continuity with the past, with the European art tradition she'd grown up with. She'd auditioned three times for minor parts at Stratford, but she didn't get even one. The idiots. Before she'd got pregnant, she acted in the Częstochowa International Festival of Plays, which made Stratford's look like a hick affair.

"But Bill, business is down fifty percent," Sabina said. "Americans aren't coming to the festival anymore. They don't want to get passports, and the border has lineups since 9/11. People don't have money. Or they're scared of losing jobs." Her lip quivered, but the Holy Mother kept her from crying. "And now I'm going to lose my house and business—what am I going to do?"

She thought of the festival volunteers she'd met, like Bill's wife Marjorie: pampered women with showy houses. People with money but no taste.

Marjorie, however, shunned the others' bourgeois flash, at least most of the time. Since her children had grown up, Marjorie—"going crazy at home with boredom and my old-fart husband," she'd said —had retrained as a nurse and worked in Stratford General Hospital's emergency department.

"Don't get me wrong," Marjorie had said, "I love Bill. He drives me nuts, but with the kids gone, I don't know what I'd do if I lost him."

As their friendship developed, Sabina and Marjorie had kept monthly lunch dates. Occasionally, they'd spend an evening at Marjorie's. Sabina had entertained her pal with soliloquies from Shakespeare, and Marjorie had regaled Sabina with tales from the hospital—stories about death, medical mistakes and mismanagement.

"Makes me fear for friends who end up in Stratford General," Marjorie had said.

Sabina always refused to have Marjorie over to her puny place. She knew what her friend would think. At a volunteer meeting held years before at Jane Brody's house, Marjorie had leaned to Sabina and whispered: "What a dump. Walls as flimsy as paper. And see that sofa? Looks like Jane bought it at Walmart." A month before the meeting, Sabina had been readying her house to open as a bed and breakfast, and she'd bought new bedroom sets at Walmart.

Bill stopped fingering his hair and picked up his coffee cup. "Unfortunately," he said, "having a B and B in this town *now* is death to one's credit rating. An extra line of credit is out of the question. But I could help in an … informal way."

Sabina noticed a leather bomber jacket hanging from a coat-hook and suppressed a smile; Bill had always been a button-down banker. Conservative suits. Pinstripes. She wondered if he'd now bought a red sports car to match his new wardrobe.

"I love Marj," Bill said. "Raising the kids, travelling, it's been great. But now she pecks at me over nothing and everything." He sighed. "You know … I've looked at you for a long time. From afar—whenever Marj has you over for coffee. How many years has that been? I've overhead you talking and been intrigued. The healing power of the icon. The House of Poetry in … Często—Częstochowa. How's my pronunciation?"

He leaned forward and grasped her hand.

"I like you, Bill." He'd always been gracious when she'd been over at Marjorie's. She liked his muscled forearms; they reminded her of the boys she knew before Borys. "But Marjorie is good friend."

Bill got up from his chair, shoved his hands in his pockets, and paced the small office.

"I feel … different … when I look at you," he said. "Young. Blessed. Connected to something beyond my pay cheque and the silly ways

Marj spends it." He stopped pacing and knelt beside her. "I don't know if this is a custom in Poland," he said and held her hand again and kissed it. "I'm going to help you with the mortgage, at least until the economy—"

"But Bill, mortgage is my responsibility. I couldn't ..." Praise the Virgin Mary, Sabina thought. Her shoulders loosened and fell.

"Nonsense. I want to help." He looked at his watch. "Sorry. Have to go. Staff meeting in five minutes. But I want to see you."

Sabina left the bank and slipped a Player's out of her purse. She'd quit smoking once for ten years, until Borys's drunken bouts began to include slaps and punches. They'd loved each other. She surveyed the street and found an alcove, the doorway to a walk-up apartment. She turned away from the sidewalk, did up the buttons on her blouse, and cried.

***

Sabina's Bed and Breakfast had run for five years since Borys died. He had little insurance, and she soon had trouble paying the bills. So she had cleaned her daughters' rooms. She had painted the walls, submitted to health and safety inspections, and started advertising.

Business bustled for the first three years. The room rates compensated for Sabina's location, a neighbourhood of faded brick houses facing Highway 8 traffic. She'd made enough money for the mortgage, upkeep, and a small profit. But the Great Recession, as the newscasters called it, and the high Canadian dollar had battered her business. She'd appealed to her daughters for loans, but they were stay-at-home moms whose husbands feared for their manufacturing jobs in Windsor and Hamilton.

Her business, however, wasn't extinct—yet. The previous week, a Toronto couple booked a room. They'd arrived yesterday, and this morning she sweated in the kitchen preparing their breakfast. She placed ham, toast, and home fries on two platters and took them out to the dining room. As she treated her guests to stories of drama school in Poland, she almost believed that business was back to normal.

When breakfast was over and the couple went upstairs for their overnight bags, Sabina waited in the entrance-way. On the hall table, the icon stood in its gilded frame. She picked it up and stroked the frame. The Virgin Mary's gold-leaf halo shone as she looked down at the child in her arms. Sabina remembered when she was twelve years old, and her mother had held her hand in the Jasna Góra Monastery. Warned her to be humble. Chaste. They'd looked up at the haloed figures in the Black Madonna icon. That day, her mother had given her a small photo of the painting.

Wooden stairs squeaked as the husband clomped down them, and Sabina jumped. She replaced the icon on the table. While the husband paid by credit card, his wife tarried on the stairway, inspecting three black-and-white photographs arranged diagonally up the wall.

"These are beautiful," the wife said.

"Yes. That's Borys, my husband. Dead now."

"I'm sorry." The wife took two steps down and pointed at the next photo. "This one—is it of you? Gorgeous."

"Thank you. I went to academy of arts—took drama. But I dropped out." Sabina patted her stomach. "Already pregnant."

Sabina looked up at the portrait of a voluptuous twenty-year-old posed in a mohair turtleneck and pencil skirt. The clothes hugged the girl's curves, and her crown of Farrah Fawcett hair glittered. The boys in Sabina's high school had fought over her, and she'd revelled in their adoration. She felt that old joy this morning with Bill. She wanted to fall in love, marry Bill, and see envy in the parochial Stratford women who raised their eyebrows at her English. But she couldn't place Marjorie in the daydream.

***

Bill and Sabina exchanged e-mail messages until they agreed on a time and place. A café or restaurant was too risky. So on a steamy evening, they met in the bank's parking lot and took his Toyota Prius to the Avon Motel, on the eastern edge of town. A sign in the parking lot promoted "family specials, 20% off during festival season" in moveable plastic letters.

At the building's entrance, Bill hiked up the black leather bag he was carrying on his shoulder and opened the door for Sabina. He signed in, took the room keys from the attendant, and gestured to Sabina. "After you. It's Room C7."

They walked down a corridor lit by brass wall sconces, and Bill unlocked C7's door. On the room's far wall, two tepid floral prints hung over a queen-size bed. Bill laid his car keys on a coffee table and poured wine from the mini-bar into plastic glasses: he passed one to Sabina. They sat on a sofa near patio doors facing an auto-body shop's brick wall. Beside the wall, fading sunlight speckled a row of maples, and blue-grey farm fields flickered in the haze.

Sabina wasn't sure what to do. She wanted to touch him. After a few minutes, Bill laid his glass on the coffee table and reached down to a bulky leather bag, which he'd placed beside the sofa, and pulled out a thick hardcover. He tilted the book's cover toward Sabina. *English Parish Churches.*

"I've heard you tell Marj you miss your church in Poland. But you attend Knox Presbyterian downtown, right?"

"Yes. Very different church from mine. But the building is big and elegant. It has good feel." Sabina wondered why—with the two of them sitting together in a motel room—Bill was so interested in what church she went to.

"Except for my kids' weddings, I haven't been in a church since I was twelve," Bill said. "Too much bullshit, pardon my French."

He opened the book and flipped through the pages. With a twinge in her chest, Sabina edged closer to him. "Well, the churches in this book aren't Polish—my background is Brit—but they're beautiful. They send me back in time."

Sabina moved still closer. Their knees touched. She felt weak, like warm wet paper. As he pointed out his favourites, she perused the pictures. Church naves with semi-circular Roman arches. Light spreading onto cold floors. Stone walls rising into gloom but pierced by arched white windows.

"These pictures remind me of you," Bill said. "Serene. Spiritual."

"You mistake me for saint," Sabina said. "I have vices."

Bill smiled. "Could you show me some of them?"

Sabina leaned her head close to Bill's and brought her lips against his. He wrapped his arms around her back, and she reached to hold his neck. A river of colours flowed through her. She didn't want to stop.

Bill pulled away and said: "I want to learn all about you, about growing up in the Polish People's Republic—everything. But there's lots of time for that." He pointed to the bottle sitting on the mini-bar fridge. "More wine?"

Walking back with the filled glasses, Bill didn't notice his leather bag by the sofa. As his left foot hit the bag, the rest of his body kept moving. Sabina shrieked. The wine glasses arced through the air, Bill sprawled forward, and his head smashed into the coffee table.

Sabina knelt down beside him, but he was unconscious, blood trickling from his right temple. Holy Mother of God! She jumped up and scanned the room for a telephone. She lurched to the bed-side table and tried calling 911, but when the call seemed to fail she slammed down the phone and stumbled along the corridor to the registration desk. The clerk made the call.

A few minutes later, two paramedics arrived in an ambulance. They followed Sabina and the clerk to room C7 and asked what had happened.

"We were just looking at a book," Sabina said and pointed to *English Parish Churches*, which still lay open on the sofa. God is punishing me, she thought. "That's all, I swear. And then Bill tripped and hit his head on table."

Sabina perched on the coffee table, leaned her head toward her chest, and rubbed her forehead with a shaky hand. She tried to hold the sound back, but the sobbing broke free.

The paramedics shrugged and turned to monitor Bill's vital signs. As they moved him onto a stretcher, the clerk walked Sabina back to the registration desk, and she stood watching as the ambulance turned from the parking lot onto Highway 8. After she grabbed Bill's keys and leather bag she thanked the clerk. Outside, her high heels clicked over the asphalt. She unlocked the Prius and got in.

Adjusting the seat- and mirror-controls, she thought, Please, Holy Mother, let Marjorie not be on duty.

***

In Stratford General's parking lot, as she got out of the Prius, Sabina saw the two paramedics wheeling Bill's stretcher through Emergency's sliding glass doors. She ran and followed them inside, almost colliding with a janitor who was mopping a corner of the floor.

Beneath the ceiling grid of acoustic panels and fluorescent lights, Marjorie approached in green scrubs, her running shoes squeaking on the white floor tiles. She recognized Sabina and smiled. But when she saw Bill, bleeding and unconscious in the stretcher, the corners of her mouth dropped. The paramedics started relaying Bill's vital signs, but Marjorie's eyes rolled back and her body slumped to the floor.

One of the paramedics, a 250-pound bull, jumped to help Marjorie; the other wheeled Bill away in search of another nurse. Ten seconds later, Marjorie stirred and tried to get up, but the paramedic held her.

"Where ... where's Bill?" Marjorie said, struggling against the paramedic's hold. "Where's my Billy?"

"Don't worry," the paramedic said, "he's being treated. You need to lie down." He guided Marjorie's back to the floor and leaned over her, loosening the nurse's clothes.

With the paramedic blocking Marjorie's view, Sabina saw her chance to escape. Moving further into Emergency, she strode through the waiting room and then along a series of corridors, finding an exit at last. When she'd navigated back to Bill's Prius, she got in and drove to the tony neighbourhood where he and Marjorie lived. She parked the car in their driveway and dropped the keys in the mail slot.

As she walked the half-hour back to her neighbourhood, she smoked a Player's, and its papery clouds obscured her sight. She imagined she was hugging Bill under the arches of Jasna Góra. As priests chanted in brocaded red-and-gold gowns, Bill kissed her in a trapezoid of light.

***

Late the next morning, Sabina struggled out of the bedclothes. When she brought her feet to the oak floorboards of her bedroom, her toes sank into a pizza of cold vomit. The knuckles and heel of her right hand hurt. They were bruised and crisscrossed with bloody cuts. She found gauze in the bathroom, applied peroxide to the cuts, and wrapped up her hand. She cleaned up the vomit, washed her feet in the bathtub, and put on her slippers and robe. Back in her bedroom, she lit a Player's, longing to vanish into its aroma.

The previous evening, after she'd walked back from Bill's, she had brought out Borys's last bottle of Sobieski, which she'd kept in the dining room cabinet since his death. She'd opened the bottle and poured herself a glass. And then another. She remembered nothing after that.

Except the icon.

She stumbled down the stairway. On the entrance-way floor-boards, the paper icon lay under a spider's web of broken glass. The Virgin's image was ripped and pulled out of its gilt frame. Sabina bent down and caressed the paper, grains of glass sticking to her fingertips.

The doorbell rang. Sabina crunched across glass shards to the front door.

Through the peep hole, Marjorie's nose looked like a knife as she stood in her green scrubs and white running shoes, her arms folded in front and her jaw locked.

After a long moment, Sabina opened the door. Marjorie glared. Sabina's shoulders shook and a hot tide burned her eyes.

"Acting now?" Marjorie said and smirked, then walked away.

The paper icon slid from Sabina's fingers.

Deluge
/Parable of the Mock-Heroic/

S.D. Chrostowska

We no doubt forget that our first experiences of reading
are physical experiences and that it is our bodily relationships
to books that may be formative of our attitudes toward
them and their uses ever afterward.

—HAYDEN WHITE

"SHHHH!" I SAID quite impatiently.

"Oh be quiet yourself! It's closing time!" Three girls giggled, hiding their mouths behind fanned fingers. Flustered, I looked away, while they resumed their Chinese whispers. The clock showed 22:45. Soon the girls turned to leave, armoured with their susurrations, and I remained, clawless, pacing in the dark.

I have seen and read too many books on too many subjects. Sources of which I cannot recall. My thirst for them is still insatiable. An absurdity perhaps: I began dozing on stacks of periodicals. I dream differently here—that's certain. I re-shelve nothing of importance, keeping it locked up with me in my carrel. I learn cumulatively, study by accumulation. *Possidere* paper. If I were to choose among sensuous riches and sensible *biblia*, which would it be? Haven't I already chosen? If I could, I'd inscribe myself on a page. My body and history, my life and times ... Yawn an O, perch on T, curl in S, break in V ... *Sui scriptoris*. A scripted slate. I am happiest in words, you realize. I understand myself better without abbreviation.

History: the milieu of books was to have the essence of knowledge and wisdom. Just being in their presence was to contain them, know them inside out. I would touch, pull, handle, let them fall apart in my hand, or split open those rarely or never opened, to stroke the paper, to finger the thickness of a page. *Obsequium.* I would bring the open face, *recto-verso*, up to my eyes to detect the height of print, and bring my nose down to guess the printer by smell alone. I would be pleased with either making a new friend, or finding an old one. Across I saw the books there, lined lopsidedly on burdened shelves, pushing against the wood, propping one another with a mutuality unknown to man. Along they were in the hermetic humidity of a tiny library, the atlases and reference volumes dry in locked glass cabinets.

Those dimensions my aunt held the keys to, those only she could keep. Aunt would be propped up stern behind her desk, cushioned in her armchair, a hand-knitted coverlet over her shoulders in colder weather, always self-same (even now—fifteen years since). The dampness of the winter months translated into something merciless and bone-chilling; in the summer the room became a rainforest, and the reading table a trail blazed with inhuman resolve. Seasons revolve within it. Plants and succulents dominate the window sills. Flowers in vases open, wither, and die. Globes rotate. This, her pulpous empire: a small space on the second storey of my elementary school, one fair-sized room turned into a maze with the aid of furniture—a vessel loaded down with priceless cargo, at anchor by Paris Commune Square, afloat on the V. river. My aunt's glasses clamp the tip of her nose, the glass fingered, unclear, behind it a concerned face drawn into a ponytail with a black rubber band, her hair auburn, but graying. And aunt has no time for me again! I patter along the shelves in contemplation of this fact, just as other children cue up before her desk at recess to borrow books. I leaf through the card-catalogue, a hairbrush in my hand, my hair tangled, awaiting her stroke. Instead, crabbed censure. Officiousness. Why not treat me as befits your niece? (Why dismiss me? *Why throw me in the river?*)

Why, together in the mornings we eat eggs and cheese or ham

on rye bread or Kaiser roll. We drink tea together, dark tea made for grown-ups, talk slightly, quarrelsomely, like the grown-ups whose tea we drink. Cold comfort. I fly out: the folded intestine of stairs still reeks of cats, piss vapour rises from the basement where the naked man waits ... I am told about him much, afraid a bit. I have never seen the man, but Uncle said he was a madman, and I believed it then and there. He may want to rape, or slit a throat, or whatnot. No telling what he'd do. Maybe he exists, but no one has seen him. I glance cravenly into the dank cellar, its gate unlocked, unlatched. Like a crypt, it lets out an audible death-sigh, the breath of dirt, the stench of urine. Prompted by my descent, a bundle of cats scurry out onto the lawn. I skip down the stairs, past windows of splintered glass, making a clamour: hear me coming!

Here I think it cruel I should leave first—while she, aunt, lingers. And Uncle leaves so early. It's already past eight and classes have begun. But see her coming to school after nine! (Those cats I mentioned dash for the broken windows of the cellar as she walks by.) But I know she is almost retired; "retired" is when one tires out once and for all, after lifelong exertion, having lost the strength to work. But in my aunt there is still a will; she has waned, but only partly. She must have rests to retrieve her peace..She has never been warm to me, only tolerant. I let my hair loose, undoing her shoddy job. I approach my makeshift bed. She shuffles past my room on her way to the couch. It is nighttime again.

[page 44]¹

Sniff scrambled under the table while Moomintroll, Snufkin and the Hemulen held the jar over the Hobgoblin's Hat, and the Snork gingerly unscrewed the lid. In a cloud of sand the Ant-lion tumbled out, and, quick as lightning, the Snork popped a Dictionary of Outlandish Words on top. Then they all dived under the table and waited.

At first nothing happened.

They peeped out from under the tablecloth, getting more and more agitated. Still there was no change.

"It was all rot," said Sniff, but at that moment the big dictionary began to crinkle up, and in his excitement, Sniff bit the Hemulen's thumb thinking it was his own.

Now the dictionary was curling up more and more. The pages began to look like withered leaves, and between them the Outlandish Words came out and began crawling around on the floor.

[page 45]

"Goodness, gracious me," said Moomintroll.

But there was more to come. Water began to drip from the brim of the hat and then to overflow and to splash down onto the carpet so that the Words had to climb up the walls to save themselves.

"The Ant-lion has only turned into water," said Snufkin in disappointment.

"I think it's the sand," whispered the Snork. "The Ant-lion is sure to come soon."

I close a book and switch off my light. I can never read more than a page at a time, though I so love reading.

* * *

—I awake next on the margin of night (is it more dawn than dusk?), not from weak dreams but from reminiscing. The room is very dry: a well like other wells, stairwells, farewells—all emptied of water, some cried out. Water is an enemy of crisp Book, that which makes it shrivel, fade, close never to reopen. I thought of water out of thirst; I need to reach the fountain outdoors, on a camel in the hall, hot and dusty and now deserted. I have read landlocked stories with plural meanings that brought sand to my eyes. I might also have read this story somewhere. If it's inchoate, it is because I'm no storyteller, no boy who rides beasts on quests for beauty. I am a bedouin, a reader of routes, and this story pertains to me only loosely.

***

How is it apparent I spend my nights here? I stay confined to a single cell within this massive honeycomb. I have been alluded to, but how have I been traced? I now know: I am brief but not invisible.

I am not alone. Another one adopted my habits and sleeps in a stall in the yellow section (while I stay on the opposite side, in the red). Oh, we have not met, but oftentimes I hear him passing through the hall, nimbly across the bare floors. Across he passes, along and among books. He must notice my feeble light to stave off intrusion. In near silence and darkness our senses stay as taut as strings, straining to see, hear, hesitant whether what is heard should not have been seen instead, and whether what was seen wasn't a sound, a voice melodious. He encroaches on my domain. Something's afoot. Is he yielding to neglected senses? Or is he after or in search of something? And are his motives decent? What is he about? I cannot help my misgiving: many people are killers at heart. And I am not a stranger to myself, I am here for another reason. I would spy to find out more about the curious fellow, yet dread an unexpected confrontation on some twist or turn in pitch-darkness. Did I not mention it is a library in which we are marooned?

The one place I cannot bear being absent from. Four discreet weeks. Four weeks since I lodged in a cubicle, having fallen asleep. I seldom stir from here, and if I do, I stay out of others' sight, moving listlessly along the rows of shelves. Then in and out, I fall, panting, down the throat of a stairwell. I jump four, six steps at a time! And all along I grasp the railing like an aerialist. Alone, then among people ... I am brief—almost invisible—because I seem very gray. Oh yes, living among books, one's complexion assumes a submerged hue. The monolith, the Kingdom of Book, is ruled by age; age by decay; decay by fading; and fading bows before the insipid colour gray. Unless there is water aflood.

***

The fellow was my spy, as I understood. Now I am licking my wounds after a fight. We struggled with each other, fought a battle at Yellow & Red—when we could have made a pact of silence ... We spoke. Should I say how? (The time approaches when my state will be made known to the staff. I shall seem bold and defiant.)

How could I have been sure that, while I was briefly away at a lecture or meal, this seat of mine wasn't soiled by the rude cipher, or worse, by a bevy of somesuch vulgar folk?

Well, somehow I was. There, I reckon, they debated me over, the rude fellow energized like an organ. Then, tuned by their scheme, he did what I had done. Well upon the hour of my return my foes had left. Crumbs hurriedly brushed off my desk by an interloper's sleeve, beverage spills wiped dry, hair shed onto the back of my chair—all gone. Any evidence? No. This is not hard to imagine.

Well, he stayed behind to find me out. Our trajectories crossed in his second week, our skulls clashing over the fountain in wet-dark.

"Who are you? I won't tell," he demanded in a volatile voice.

I made no reply.

"Aha! Comrade I know you! I have read your crime back to back!"

That was when I raved:

"I will bring water aflooding! Rescue no one! Alone, afloat, I will appear among people!"

We clutched each other's throats and clenched our teeth, our noses bloody, our ears torn, our hair yanked out in tufts. We fought an awful, clawful fight—it seemed to the death. When water sprang up, rising with a show of might, filling the tower like a tank, not one book was spared or salvaged. The kingdom and spy disappeared underwater. And after the scene had settled, I, the victor, merely drifted across, along the walls, picking up washed words, nodding to myself.

---

1. Italicized fragment comes from *Finn Family Moomintroll* by Tove Jansson, given here in Ernest Benn's translation.

THE GOD OF BABY BIRDS

Zoe C. Greenberg

I GREW UP in Brilsk, in Southeast Poland, a town of round yellow cheeses and girls in braids. My earliest memory is white window squares, silent and glowing. Mama said it was so cold the winter I was born, the frost on the glass did not clear until late April, when the ice on the Dunajec finally cracked.

Only two women in Brilsk had babies that long winter. Leja was born first, a few fields away, in the big house her grandparents built. Brilsk was the centre of a big state dairy, where our fathers worked as engineers—my Tata on the generators, and Mr. Stolarski, the irrigation. In 1961, they still believed that agricultural development would make our future.

Every month they walked together to the great hall to make reports to the regional conference of the Polish United Worker's Party. The meetings went late into the night, lights blazing, until they walked home in the dark, finished with talking. They made a real pair: my father, small and quick, beside him Mr. Stolarski, slow and big like a bear.

I remember Leja in our classroom. She sits at the front, with her long red braids and her starched blue shorts, paying close attention. Her face is smudged in my memory, as if painted by a Chinese brush. Quickly she raises her hand, wanting to be chosen. Mama said Leja was a bright girl, I should be careful she didn't fool me. And she whispered, there's no denying the Jew in her.

But how could I think that way? Leja's family were the last Jews in Brilsk, so what did that mean? After school we met at the great boulder between our fields, and wandered the tractor road as far as it would go. We passed groves of thin, young trees; an old cistern, filled with algae; rusted threshing blades. Everywhere were flocks of birds, disturbed by our exploring. We knew they were nothing like us, but we loved them. They were so alive, so shiny; they would not let us touch their bodies. Sometimes they looked at us with tiny black eyes, and their minds came through.

Once we climbed a tree and found a nest of dead eggs. Why had the mother abandoned them? Did the noise of the combines come too close? Was it too easy for foxes to reach, the nest too bare to the winds? Then down on the ground beside it, a baby bird. Eyes swollen, mouth open with its last cry. We took it to the great boulder, to perform a ceremony to the God of Birds. A God we had just discovered. A God who would take this tiny life.

Leja held my hand. She told me how her mother had said an angel was born when two people become friends, and the angel watches over them, blessing them with laughter. But if the friends are separated for more than a year, that angel will die. And when they see each other again, the friends must say a prayer for the angel, like a prayer for the dead. And she spoke the prayer in her Jewish language.

I knew that could never happen. A year was impossible! We were floating in the long dream of childhood, the age when your head smells like sugar. Pink and newborn, the angel of our friendship rose above us, and all across the fields of Brilsk, on every branch in every tree, the sky was filled with the songs of baby birds.

***

When I was a girl on the Brilsk dairy farm, our mothers bragged we were so healthy. But this was because we spent most of our time outdoors, away from our parents. The adults were grey, they took twice as long to do the same things, their limbs were heavy. They did not know they were living with a terrible disease, the disease of despair. We sensed they would poison us if we listened to them. So we slipped away, running to the fields, coming back at sundown with dirty knees.

Our secret home, we called it. Out there we were Badger and Rabbit, no longer Leja and Weronika. Like all good communist children, we believed in the workers' party. But in our secret home, we were royalty.

One warm day at the riverbank, we lay on mossy rock, looking up at dense leaves. Leja turned her face to stare at the water. I followed her gaze to where the sunlight fell on the surface and shattered into a million fragments. I was suddenly afraid. "Are you angry at me?" I asked.

Leja did not smile. She began to speak, slowly and softly. She wanted to make a change to our secret home. Everything would be the same, she said. Except she wouldn't be Jewish anymore, she'd just be a regular girl.

She said how the night before, her whole family had gone to Olga Cykowska's house, and Mr. Cykowski had come to pick them up in his car, the fancy one he got for being Regional Secretary. They rode over in this special Swiss Fiat, and there were lots of fried potatoes, and after dinner she sang a folk song for everyone, and Mrs. Cykowska said she was charming.

Then the kids were allowed to go play. Olga had a kitten, a fuzzy grey thing from the barns, but she wouldn't let Leja hold it. She kept grabbing it out of her hands. And Olga wouldn't let Leja's brother play with her wooden train cars either. So when Olga turned to grab the train cars from Paweł, Leja took the kitten and put it on her back, to ride Olga like a donkey. They all laughed, but Olga cried and the cat was scared and scratched her, deep in the skin.

Mrs. Cykowska was very angry. "What's wrong with you?" she shouted.

They had to walk all the way home, in their fancy shoes. All the way home, and no words.

In the living room, Leja's mother went up to her bedroom right away, but Mr. Stolarski sat with Leja.

"Leja, my sweet, you know we are dedicated socialists. We owe the

Party everything. We thank the Party for my job, for eating well, so much better than the lady could feed us during the war, in the cellar with the potato peels. The Party gave us citizen rights, and sent me to engineering, even though I was a Jew. That's why we are grateful to Secretary Cykowski. That's why being of Jewish origin means we have to approach things differently. Do you understand? We have to behave well. Friendships matter to us more than they do to them."

That's when Leja decided that in our secret home, there would be no Jews. We would all be Poles. In our secret forest home, everyone was the same, everyone was friends, and every night there was only dancing together.

***

Shortly after I saw Mr. Stolarski sitting in our parlour. Mama poured him tea, and Tata leaned towards him, frowning. He had the same expression on his face from when he was doing a riddle.

Mr. Stolarski was mounded on the couch like mashed potatoes. He spoke rapidly, in the loud whisper adults used for secrets. I had many times seen him sit across from my father, preoccupied with mathematics or puzzles, but they made only grunts. Now he was like Leja—a river tumbling from his mouth. I wondered if this was the way all Jews spoke, quickly rushing from point to point. Maybe this is why Mama was afraid.

My father interrupted this torrent. "There's no choice, Stolarski." It was his normal speaking voice, yet it seemed he shouted.

Mama caught me watching. "The walls have ears," she warned.

Tata sighed and rubbed his face with his hands. Stolarski sat back silent and would not look at me.

I understood I had done something wrong and scrambled up the stairs, not knowing the punishment. The adults could hiss all day—I opened my book and fell into reading. I wanted to be just like Tata, surrounded only by books. I believed what he said, that words would make a better future.

***

Later Tata climbed the ladder to my bedroom. He sat with me and stroked my hair until I finished the chapter.

"How would you feel," he asked, "if Leja came to live with us?"

I dropped my book to the floor. "Tato! She can sleep with me?"

"Of course." My father smiled.

"Is something wrong with the Stolarskis?"

"There's luck. They're going to Canada."

Canada. A land of pine trees, lakes, and igloos. "But won't Leja be lonely without her mama?"

"It's just for a while, to get things ready. Then she can join them. Don't tell your friends—if it becomes gossip the Stolarskis are leaving, and Leja is waiting behind, they won't be very nice. Do you understand?" His even, handsome face looked at me closely.

I did, the way I understood that some books in his study were off-limits, that no one should know about Mama's sewing machine, that what Mama and Tata whispered to each other must never be repeated. Secrets were an essential part of life, a tool to divide some parts of the grown-up world from others: Tata had private books, Mama's friends wore clothing she made for them. And now Leja, my best friend, my new sister, was living with us.

***

I was afraid Leja might be sad without her family, but immediately she was cooking with Mama—flour and heat and constant mixing. Still I preferred Tata's library. There I could explore his many books, neatly numbered according to his invented system. I went there to learn his secrets, opening them all, even the technical manuals—there was science, philosophy, poetry, even Russian, the strange Cyrillic letters marching across the page like tiny beetles.

All that winter I sat cozy with Tata, while Leja and my mother worked in the kitchen. She called me Husband and I called her Wife and we laughed. Sometimes I still called her Badger, and she called me big clumsy Rabbit, but there was a new feeling between us as the snow closed over the fields of Brilsk. Sharing the same bedroom, we were together even when quiet; now our connection became wordless. A glance could say everything. Womanhood was near us, everyone said, something serious about husbands and babies, but we were happy in our little attic, snuggling together while the ice froze over the trembling grasses on the banks of the Dunajec.

Sometimes we would kiss and caress. With Leja, in the attic of the house in Brilsk. It was not for sex, but the opposite: to stay hidden in the world of children.

***

After the Stolarskis had been gone a few months, spring slowly unwrapped the blanket of snow from our village. We broke from the house and into the muddy fields like before. Leja remembered a lilac tree growing beside her father's workshop, and wanted to see the gigantic blossoms. She said they hung over a rooftop where we could climb and sit.

Leja's house was watched by Isaac, her uncle from Kraków, who came twice a month to make it look like the Stolarskis were still there. There could be jealousy if someone had a visa to the West. At that time only Jews could leave—the Party had ordered them out, saying they were a foreign element. Tata and the co-op engineers knew the Stolarskis had gone to Canada, but the others only guessed. Their house was suspect, marked, like a sore that some in our village would like to scratch. Left empty, it could be ruined by drunken boys or vandals. And then what would happen to Leja?

Isaac was unshaven and muttered to himself, and we hoped to avoid him, so we walked carefully past the house to the workshop. We could see the blooms bright as grapes in the thick green foliage. It was easy to crawl up the slope behind the shed, and only a little scary to leap over the gap to the roof. We lay on the rough black shingles, the hot tar warming our backs, the new spring sunlight coming through the clouds and baking our sweaters.

The lilac smell was so strong it made us silent. I closed my eyes for a moment, breathing in, then opened to the thick, padded sky above. "Rain," I said.

"Then we work quick." Leja reached up to pull down a lilac bloom. The thin branches were young and green and the purple flowers tickled our faces. "Like this."

She gently pulled a little blossom from its stem and put the base between her lips. Then she quickly sucked in, her eyes lighting up. She blew out, spitting the flower into my face. "Sweet," she said, laughing.

I took hold of a nearby bloom and drew the scent to my face. Gently I pulled one of the flowers and sucked on the little opening, as Leja showed me, to feel a sudden burst of nectar on the tip of my tongue.

"We'll never need food again!" I cried.

"We can run away, and still eat!"

Heaven, we named it, a shelter of green glowing leaves and scent, the most sacred of sacred places. I don't think, in all my life, I ever felt peace like that. Under the lilac tree in Spring. We lay talking and drinking the bursts of nectar until the air around us grew deep blue and the birds in the tree above began to sing so loud we could hardly hear each other. Then we walked slowly home, looking for more food at every step. We were chewing wild chives when I found a huge orange mushroom growing on a tree, but as always, Leja was smart and stopped me from biting.

***

Summer came and the air grew stuffy and sour in our house. Mama had become more and more angry—as if she expected me to be wild and defiant, a totally different person. Her words were short, spitting. She was like water on a skillet. Nothing I could do right.

To retaliate, I refused to do chores, but she gave me such a slap in the face. I wept in my bed, confused, afraid of Mama, and did not believe she loved me.

If only I could run forever with Leja to our secret home, bury myself in her arms, breathe and forget everything. But she also changed. As the summer passed, her eyes grew quiet. She wore the same dress for a week, not caring how she smelled, and did not invent new dishes. She did not meet me at the great boulder, but went immediately to the kitchen, whispering gossip with my mother. The strangest was that she grew thick and strong, as if her father's body had been hiding in her. Now we both were bigger, and the bed we shared grew tighter.

One day a letter arrived for Tata from Canada, with another, smaller letter inside. Leja snatched it from my father's hands and ran off to the fields. I let her go, and stayed to watch Tata.

When he was done reading he put down the letter. He rubbed his eyes slowly, his glasses falling onto his lap. Then he yawned, a huge crack of jaw, and, tucking his hands under his armpits, stared at me blankly.

"Mr. Stolarski is sending money for Leja next week. She's going to take a train to Italy and relatives, and from there, join the family in Israel."

I felt cold over my body. "I thought they were in Montreal."

"Mr. Stolarski has a cousin in Israel who can help them get a big apartment. You know, it will be easier for Leja to pass to Vienna if she says she's going to Israel. They'll be happy to let her go."

"And why shouldn't she be with her own kind?" my mother said, who I hadn't noticed listening.

"We are her kind!" I shouted. "What's in Israel? Nothing on the news but tanks and sand!"

Tata looked at me carefully. "Nothing will happen to her in Israel," he said.

My mother walked towards me, putting her hands heavily on

my shoulders. She looked into my face, then held my cheeks in her palms. "Weronika," she said, "everyone has their own path in life."

I ran to my room, my throat tight. Under the covers alone and suffocating in that little grey house.

***

But for Leja it was happy news. We sat together in our attic, the afternoon sun filling the room with a warm golden glow, while she told me all about it. They would live in Haifa, a quiet university town. They arranged for her first to take school in Polish, and learn Hebrew at night. There was even a culinary institute. There she could make her dream of owning a restaurant. And Haifa was beautiful, with beaches, palm trees, and different exotic kinds of people from all over the world.

"All Jews?" I asked.

Leja stroked aside my bangs. "I should trim your hair before I go," she said.

"Leja!" Mama called from the kitchen. "Please come do your potatoes." Leja stood to go downstairs, then turned to look at me.

"Yes, all Jews," she said, and did not hide her smile.

I thought about the angel of our friendship, and her prayer. Maybe if I believed enough in God, we wouldn't be apart for longer than a year. But something else was pulling on me, something that can break a heart and also free it. Something between letting go and betraying. I looked at Leja's face, growing solid now, with adult shapes beneath her cheeks.

Outside the attic window, we heard a raven cawing over the garden. The sun had left the room and all that remained was furniture. Leja turned to go, and like always, I followed close behind.

Acknowledgements

"Deluge" by S.D. Chrostowska appeared in *The Review of Contemporary Fiction* 33.1 (2013).

A longer version of "Rosetta" by David Huebert appeared in *Grain* 41.2.

"Polish Wedding" by Katherine Koller is recently published (in a slightly different version) as a chapter in the novel, *Art Lessons* (Great Plains, 2016) as "Trees Entwined."

A shorter version of "The Bear" by Katarzyna Jaśkiewicz was a part of a novel *Ogród Króla Agrestów* (*Garden of the Gooseberry King*), published in Poland by Wydawnictwo Poligraf in 2012.

"The Tower of Fools" by Małgorzata (Margaret) Nowaczyk has been published in Numero Cinq, August 2016. http://numerocinq magazine.com/2016/08/06/tower-fools-margaret-nowaczyk/

"Happily Ever After" by Corinne Wasilewski appeared *The Windsor Review*, Fall 2010, Volume 42, Number 2, pp. 44-55.

"Paper Icon" by Robert B. Young appeared in *Other Voices*, Volume 23, Number 2, Spring 2011, (Edmonton: The Other Voices Publishing Society) pp. 28-38.

Author Biographies

MARK BONDYRA is a Vancouver-based writer and designer. He is currently working on a collection of short stories and a novel. In his free time he climbs mountains.

ANDREW J. BORKOWSKI's story collection, *Copernicus Avenue*, is set in Toronto's Polish community. It won the 2012 Toronto Book Award and was shortlisted for the 2012 Danuta Gleed Literary Award.

CHRISTIJAN ROBERT BROERSE studied philosophy and German at Brock University. He lived for a spell in British Columbia. His poetry has appeared in Canadian journals. He is currently learning Polish.

JOWITA BYDLOWSKA is a journalist and an author of a bestselling memoir, *Drunk Mom*, and a novel, *Guy*. She lives in Toronto, Canada.

S.D. CHROSTOWSKA teaches at York University and is the author of three books—*Literature on Trial* (University of Toronto Press, 2012), *Permission* (Dalkey Archive, 2013), and *Matches* (punctum, 2015)—and co-editor of *Political Uses of Utopia* (Columbia University Press, 2016).

Poet and actor **ZOE GREENBERG**'s experimental films have been shown in New York, Dublin, and St. Petersburg. She lives in Montreal with her husband, a painter, and their son.

DAVID HUEBERT's first book of poetry was published by Guernica in 2015. His fiction won first prize in *The Antigonish Review* and *The Dalhousie Review*'s 2015 short story contests and the 2016 CBC Short Story Prize. His debut short fiction collection, *Peninsula Sinking*, will be published by Biblioasis in 2018.

KASIA JARONCZYK immigrated to Canada in her teens, in 1992. She is a microbiologist by training. Her writing was published in *Bristol Prize Anthology* 2016, *Room, Carousel, Nashwaak Review, Prairie Journal, Room,* and *Postscripts to Darkness.* Her short story collection *Lemons* will be published by *Mansfield Press* in 2017.

KATARZYNA JAŚKIEWICZ, journalist, teacher and writer, came to Canada in 1984. She has published two novels: *Niepamięć* (Feniks award, longlisted for Cogito award) and *Ogród Króla Agrestów.* She lives in Toronto.

KATHERINE KOLLER is an Edmonton playwright (*The Seed Savers, Last Chance Leduc, Riverkeeper*). Other excerpts from her novel, *Art Lessons* (Great Plains, 2016), have appeared in *Alberta Views, Room,* and *National Voices.*

DAWID KOŁOSZYC is a poet, essayist, and short prose writer. Born in Poland, he currently lives in Montreal, where he teaches humanities at Vanier College.

AGA MAKSIMOWSKA is the author of the novel *Giant,* a finalist for the 2013 Toronto Book Award. Her writing has been published in *Brick, Rhubarb Magazine, The Globe and Mail,* and elsewhere.

LISA MCLEAN's short fiction has appeared most recently in *This* magazine, *The Antigonish Review,* and *Room.* Lisa is a freelance writer based in Guelph, Ontario.

ANNA MIODUCHOWSKA neé Wojno came to Canada at the age of thirteen. Her credits include two poetry collections, as well as publication in literary journals, anthologies, and translations. Her work has aired on radio and appeared on buses.

PAMELA MULLOY has had short fiction published in the UK and Canada, and is the editor of *The New Quarterly*. She lived in Poland for three years in the early nineties. Her debut novel, *The Deserters* (Véhicule Press), will be out in 2017.

LILIAN NATTEL is the author of *Web of Angels* (Random House 2012), *The Singing Fire* and *The River Midnight*. She lives in Toronto with her husband and two daughters.

MAŁGORZATA (MARGARET) NOWACZYK came to Canada in 1981 as a teenager. Her books *Poszukiwanie przodków* and *Rodzinne drzewo zdrowia* were published in Poland. Her short stories and essays have appeared in *Prairie Fire, Numero Cinq,* and *Geist*.

NORMAN RAVVIN's fiction publications include *The Joyful Child* (Gaspereau), *Lola by Night* and *Sex, Skyscrapers and Standard Yiddish* (paperplates books). A native of Calgary, he lives in Montreal.

DOUGLAS SCHMIDT lives in Toronto and is completing his MFA in creative writing through UBC. He has attended writing workshops at Sage Hill, the Banff Centre, and Humber College.

EVA STACHNIAK, award-winning author of historical fiction, came to Canada from Poland in 1981. Her latest novel, *The Chosen Maiden*, is inspired by the art and voice of Bronislava Nijinska.

MAGDA STROIŃSKA teaches linguistics at McMaster University in Hamilton, Ontario. Her research includes the issues of identity in exile, aging and bilingualism, political propaganda, and narratives of trauma.

ANIA SZADO, one of "Ten Canadian Women You Need to Read" (CBC), is the bestselling author of the novels *Studio Saint-Ex* and *Beginning of Was*. She lives in Hamilton, Ontario.

CORINNE WASILEWSKI lives in Sarnia. She visits Poland with her husband and has a weakness for sernik. Her novel *Live from the Underground* was published by Mansfield Press in 2015.

ROBERT B. YOUNG's short fiction has appeared in *Great Lakes Review*, *Postscripts to Darkness*, and *Other Voices*. He studied architecture in Vancouver during the 1980s, currently lives in Guelph, Ontario, and is working on his second novel.